ATOMIC ROAD

D0771432

Atomic Road

A NOVEL BY
GRANT BUDAY

ANVIL PRESS / CANADA

Anvil Press Publishers Inc.
P.O. Box 3008, Main Post Office
Vancouver, B.C. V6B 3X5 CANADA
www.anvilpress.com

Library and Archives Canada Cataloguing in Publication

Buday, Grant, 1956-, author
        Atomic road / Grant Buday. -- First edition.

ISBN 978-1-77214-113-9 (softcover)

        I. Title.

PS8553.U444A93 2018   C813'.54   C2018-901146-7

Printed and bound in Canada
Cover design by Rayola Graphic Design
Cover Photograph provided by Atomcentral.com/Peter Kuran
Interior by HeimatHouse
Represented in Canada by Publishers Group Canada
Distributed by Raincoast Books

Canadä

The publisher gratefully acknowledges the financial assistance of the Canada Council for the Arts, the Canada Book Fund, and the Province of British Columbia through the B.C. Arts Council and the Book Publishing Tax Credit.

"No one has written about me at any length, though some of my failings were discussed in the reviews of my Miró book—and I do get referred to, rather unfavourably on the whole, in an occasional article or book."

— CLEMENT GREENBERG

"I intend to stick closely to the facts...but hallucinations are also facts."

— LOUIS ALTHUSSER

ACKNOWLEDGMENTS

Atomic Road could never have been conceived much less written without John O'Brian. The concept was entirely his. Others helped, especially my wife Eden, as excellent an advocate, advisor, and editor as anyone could wish.

FOREWORD

A MISPLACED INQUIRY provided the impetus for this book. What did I know, a friend asked, about a trip to Saskatchewan by the French Marxist philosopher Louis Althusser? Nothing, I replied. Althusser never visited Canada, let alone Saskatchewan. Perhaps they had mistaken the philosopher for Lawrence Alloway, an art curator at the Guggenheim Museum in New York. Alloway had flown to Saskatchewan in 1965 to lead a workshop at an artists' retreat north of Saskatoon, in the small community of Emma Lake. Althusser stayed home in Paris.

Once the idea took root that Althusser might have visited Saskatchewan, I could not shake it. Saskatchewan had the only elected socialist government in North America, I reasoned, and he might have wanted to observe prairie socialism at firsthand, especially as some of the province's social programs were paid for with profits from uranium mining. Althusser thought nuclear weapons were more influential during the Cold War than economic issues. He might also have known that Saskatchewan was experimenting with radical new psychiatric treatments for mental illness.

Here, I thought, was the beginning of a story. The playwright Tom Cone once advised me to write about what I fear, providing me with license to start investigating nuclear events and imagery. The titles of my publications read like a radioactive laundry list: "Editing Armageddon," "Through a Radioactive Lens," *Atomic Postcards*, "On Photographing a Dirty Bomb," "Nuclear Flowers of Hell." But the books and essays are written as history, not as fiction. To tell a story about Althusser in Canada, a novelist would be required, preferably one with gallows humor.

I have thought for some while that threats to the planet produced by advanced technologies—nuclear devastation, climate change, species extinction—have grown too large to control. Despite scientific claims to the contrary, the risks can no longer be managed, but they can sometimes be made visible. Radiation cannot be seen, tasted, touched or smelled, but images of Fukushima Daiichi reveal what an exclusion zone looks like after a meltdown. There are no people. In Edward Burtynsky's photographs of uranium tailing ponds in Ontario, there are no living trees. A nuclear event, I concluded, should be part of the story. The Cuban Missile Crisis had brought the world to the brink of catastrophe around the time Althusser might have traveled to Saskatchewan, and also had the merit of coinciding with a visit to the province by Clement Greenberg, the New York art critic. Greenberg was pursued by demons, I discovered later when collaborating with him, and the same was true of Althusser. In an ill-fated way, the two intellectuals seemed to belong in the same book together.

Champion of abstract painting, Jewish intellectual, lapsed Marxist, Cold Warrior—Greenberg had been invited to Emma Lake as the workshop leader in 1962. He decided to drive across the continent rather than fly from New York. I imagined Althusser sitting in the passenger seat of Greenberg's car, gazing out the window at the passing billboards and gas stations of roadside America, while on the radio President Kennedy spoke in his Boston accent about Soviet missile installations in Cuba and impending nuclear crisis. Althusser and Greenberg would have differed, I thought, on which nation was at fault in the crisis, the philosopher siding with Khrushchev and the art critic with Kennedy. But they would have agreed that the road being traveled was dangerous. Time might be short. The clock on the dashboard of their car, like the Doomsday Clock, was inching towards midnight.

The most compelling reason for Althusser to visit Saskatchewan was to undergo psychiatric treatment. After being interned in a German prisoner of war camp for most of the Second World War, Althusser suffered episodes of mental illness for the remainder of his life. He strangled his wife in the bedroom of their apartment in Paris one Sunday morning, breaking her windpipe. He was declared unfit to stand trial on grounds of insanity and committed to Saint-Anne's psychiatric hospital.

Saskatchewan offered experimental psychiatric treatment. The mental hospital in Weyburn was internationally known for its innovative approach to mental illness. In the 1950s and 1960s, it specialized in the use of hallucinogenic drugs, particularly LSD, to treat schizophrenia. To describe the sensations induced by the drug, a doctor at the hospital coined the term psychedelic while corresponding with the novelist Aldous Huxley, who was experimenting with LSD. Huxley popularized the term in *The Doors of Perception*, a short book about his visionary experiences under the influence. "There are things known and there are things unknown," Huxley wrote, "and in between are the doors of perception." Fast forward half a century, and Donald Rumsfeld is talking about the space between nuclear known knowns and nuclear unknown unknowns in Iraq.

Althusser may have read *The Doors of Perception*. In an attempt to deal with his mental instability, he once submitted to a drug-induced narcosis, though without noticeable benefit. A journey to Weyburn to undergo LSD treatment was not out of the question, especially if someone accompanied him, and a book about his journey might succeed if the right collaborator were found. The book needed an accomplished novelist with an eye for the absurd and an ear for dialogue. Grant Buday has both.

— John O'Brian
Vancouver, July 2017

ATOMIC ROAD

Monday, 22 October, 1962

Greenberg unscrewed the latch-cap on his flask and gave it a swirl. The slip-slap warned that not much remained. He endured a moment of panic. Liquor laws, what a country. In France you could get a drink anywhere any time, but here in the US it was as if Prohibition never ended. He offered himself a sober salute in the mirror and then, rather than watch himself sip his Johnnie Walker Red at eleven on a Monday morning in the washroom of a Shell station, he shut his eyes and thought of the Shell logo, a scallop, symbol of St. James and the pilgrimage to Santiago de Compostela, because he was setting out on a pilgrimage of his own.

He took another sip. Each drink was a sandbag slumped into place to keep back the rising water—fifty-three years old and among much else he'd become a connoisseur of numbness. Opening his eyes he gazed upon the splendour of his surroundings, the red cement walls, the sink, the soap, the towel dispenser, and the toilet. Was Duchamp too obvious? Should gas station art enhance the lavatory experience or transcend it? He saw the beginnings of an essay.

A thumping at the door. Flushing the toilet, he ran water into the sink and then tipped up the flask again catching the sweet and purifying burn of the last drop on his tongue. He squared his shoulders and smoothed his hair, or what there was of it. As Greenberg stepped out, Jean Claude shoved past and slammed the door. So much for Gallic charm; it was going to be a long ride.

Straightening his coat and looking around, he discovered that the oil stains on the dirt were not uninteresting. He framed

them in his mind's eye, the bottle caps and gravel adding texture to the blue and yellow whorls seeping like mandalas into
the ground. This side of the Shell station smelled of gas, tarmac, and tires. Stepping around the corner, thinking of getting
his camera, he saw Althusser in the front passenger seat of the
Dodge gesturing for him to hurry. Greenberg was confused.
He looked back at the washroom door then again at Althusser.

"We go!"

Greenberg spotted a post, six-by-six and maybe a yard
long, and understood that this post was no mere chunk of
wood but an opportunity. The question was whether or not
he could make the most of this opportunity, whether he had
the brass. Whisky and possibility simmered in his skull. Jean
Claude would not be pleased. The toilet flushed. No, not
pleased at all. Greenberg grabbed up the post—heavy and
stinking of creosote—wedged it up under the door knob then
stood back ready to exult in Jean Claude's frustration. Unfor-
tunately the door opened inward and the post dropped onto
Jean Claude's toe. He was wearing desert boots, tan suede,
soft and supple. He was a big man, Jean Claude, six-two,
square-shouldered, a former commando, an officer in the
Resistance who'd later spent years in Algeria and Indochina.
Now he crumpled to the floor and rolled clutching his foot,
ruining his white shirt and swearing in French.

Greenberg fled for the car.

⚓

Althusser cranked down the passenger side window and held
the map out with his right arm letting it flap frantically.

At the wheel, Greenberg could see the Frenchman enjoying
the map's panic, that to him it wasn't a map at all but a swan
or an albatross.

Althusser spread his fingers wide, flung them apart in a gesture rich in brio and disdain, and the map scudded away in a tumble of white. Twiddling his fingers toodle-oo, he cranked the window up.

In the mirror Greenberg watched the map get sucked back out of view and imagined Eurydice lost to Hades. "You realize that was our road map."

"Maps are for sheep. We proceed via the pelvis." He gave a hump with his hips.

Greenberg didn't need to see things like that, what he needed was another drink, but had to settle for a cigarette. He pushed the lighter in, took his Camels from his shirt pocket, shook one up and drew it out with his lips.

"Your JFK promises to put a man on the moon by 1969," said Althusser. "I want to be this man."

Taking his attention off the road for a second Greenberg looked at the frail fortyish academic: limp-haired, slack-skinned, satchels under his eyes. When they'd rendezvoused a few days ago at the Cedar Tavern, Althusser had not walked but shuffled. Sure, he was jet-lagged, yet along with round shoulders and poor posture he breathed like the survivor of a gas attack. Now, in spite of the unseasonable October heat, he wore weighty brown tweed. An astronaut? He was a madman, and it was a miracle that such a raving Marxist had been allowed into the country. Greenberg never knew whether Althusser was being absurd or sincere or if the man even knew the difference. The lighter popped out and he pressed the glowing coil to the tip of his Camel and sucked hard. The tobacco seethed and hot smoke filled his chest. Fortified, he pressed the accelerator feeling the tidal pull of the v8.

They shot past a billboard for Kent cigarettes showing a man and woman on a golf course. Greenberg had never golfed. Maybe in the right company he'd have given it a try,

but Hemingway aside artists and intellectuals were not ath-
letic—violent drunks occasionally—but rarely sports types.

Althusser sang to the billboard, "Kiss my rooty-patooty
bebe!" Then he turned to Greenberg and said sincerely, "I like
this language very much."

"English?"

"So tactile. You can chew it. If you are lost in the desert
you can eat and drink this language and live a long time. But
it is a thief, too," he warned. "An imperialist. It steals from
the Greek and the Latin, from the Arabic and the Mandarin.
Everything it touches it takes."

Greenberg considered this. Text and Empire, Anglo-Saxon
aggression and Latinate rationality...

Althusser pulled a fuzzy, black-and-yellow striped cloth
from his coat pocket, stretched it, then fit his forefinger inside.
"It is some sort of condom, no? What big ones you Americans
think you have."

"A tiger tail," said Greenberg. "Advertising. An ornament.
You tie it to the car aerial. Put a tiger in your tank."

"Tony the Tiger."

"No, that's Frosted Flakes."

"Porky the Pig, Bugs the Bunny, Daffy the Duck, Smokey
the Bear," recited Althusser as though conjugating a verb.

They'd been on the road three hours. New York City was
behind them and now fields of dead corn stretched away on
either side and insects burst like paint pellets on the windshield. Greenberg turned a knob and a whitish fluid ejacu-
lated over the window and then the wipers stroked it away.

"If only it were so easy to clean my memory," lamented
Althusser.

"Yes," said Greenberg, who could only imagine Althusser's
burden. *Only imagine*... What a phrase. Imagination was
man's crowning faculty, the source of all art and science, and

yet to *only imagine* implied its inadequacy compared to the so-called *real thing*. He brooded and devoted himself to smoking and driving. The blue Dodge Dart Seneca was a rental, sleek and finned, with three-on-the-tree.

"Last night I dream of John Glenn and Yuri Gagarin. They are together, holding hands in space, floating, making the spiral, making the snow flake. You see, even I am not immune to the virus of melodrama. It is everywhere, like a poison gas. On the moon I will be free of memories. Without gravity there is no memory." Althusser stated this as if from personal experience.

"I dreamed last night of wood grain and sand dunes and hieroglyphics," said Greenberg. He was lying, he rarely even remembered his dreams, and hearing the dreams of others made him feel as though he lacked something fundamental, something vital.

They passed another billboard. Frigidaire Dishwashers.

"A kitsch and zinc culture," said Althusser, smug with his pun. Arm extended he examined his nails, fingers spread as if his hand was a low-flying bird, tipping it left then right as if banking side-to-side on a thermal.

Greenberg imagined those knuckly fingers around the throat of Hélène Rytman, the thumbs pressing down on her carotid arteries. Enduring a spasm of fear and nausea, and perhaps a touch of excitement, Greenberg asked, "You think we went a bit far?"

"This is a nice road," observed Althusser. "Very smooth. Good colour. I think in America you have the best roads. Except for the German roads. And the Dutch. The Dutch have very good roads. Yes, there will be anger. Jean Claude will feel unloved."

Greenberg said, "He has the charm of a jackboot."

"He is a man of duty. It is his assignment to guard me. But he is tiresome."

"A cyborg," said Greenberg.

"Someday we will all be cyborgs," stated Althusser. As ever, his tone was hard to judge; did the prospect please or displease him? "Sharper eyes, stronger hearts, bones that do not break, and of course bigger and harder erections." He grinned at this and then plunged into solemnity. "And perhaps an aversion to violence." His hands now sat like shaved rodents in his lap.

"You've been thinking about this."

"I think about everything. It is my curse."

Greenberg was frightened. "He'll catch up with us." Squinting into the dashboard-mounted mirror he expected to see Jean Claude racing up behind them in another car, shaking his fist. What he saw instead was himself: male pattern baldness, thick lips, bluish bags under his eyes—though an undeniably smooth olive complexion.

"But of course he will catch up. He is trained."

"Like a dog."

"He is a product. A widget. Is this the word, widget?" Althusser spoke an adventurous English.

"Sure."

"Or a cog. Yes, a cog. This is a good Anglo-Saxon word. Jean Claude is a cog in the machine. We fear and we admire the machine. This is so ever since Hephaestus built the first robot. The man of metal, the will of steel, the heart of gold, the cock of brass. So it is not Jean Claude's fault," Althusser said. Then he was grinning with sly satisfaction. "I wonder whose fault I am. Do you think they can cure me? Replace my broken cogs with new ones all bright and shiny?"

Greenberg hoped not. "Of course," he said. Again he mourned the empty flask in his coat pocket. Taking a long last drag on his smoke he crushed it in the ashtray then slid it shut. It closed with a satisfying click. It was a satisfying car, admirably detailed, everything fitted with craft and precision. In Manhattan he didn't need a car. He hadn't driven in a year and missed the visceral experience of raw physical force in the same way he missed sex.

"You Americans," said Althusser, pleased and patronizing.

Greenberg indulged him. "We'll cure everything, even entropy."

Althusser gurgled in joy at such hubris. "This American empire will have such a fall. At least the Romans did not deny death. Nor the Greeks or the Persians. They were realists. But you..." He sneered fondly at such an incorrigibly adolescent culture. "And your historians will weep like the children they are," he said as though reciting an elegy. Growing wistful, he let his fingers meander over the dashboard—his hand leapt as if shocked when he bumped the radio knob causing a voice to erupt like some freed imp.

"...fellow citizens..."

Kennedy's Boston twang. A replay of last night's address to the nation.

"This government, as promised, has maintained the closest surveillance of the Soviet military build-up on the island of Cuba. Within the past week, unmistakable evidence has established the fact that a series of offensive missile sites is now in preparation on that imprisoned island."

Althusser said, "They say Kennedy has syphilis."

Greenberg, indignant at such slander against his president, retorted, "They say Castro fucks chickens."

Althusser raised his chin and his eyebrows in an expression that said tell me more.

"And Khrushchev grew up fucking pigs." Greenberg had this from someone who knew someone who'd been at a costume party where J. Edgar Hoover had put in an appearance dressed as Carmen Miranda.

"Yes," murmured Althusser, "very possibly. But it is only a scandal to you Americans. I will tell you something. In France, Hugh Hefner, he would win election as president by, how do you call it, the landslide."

Greenberg envisioned Hef in the Oval Office with Playboy bunnies draped over him like ermine stoles. The State of the Union address would be given in a state of undress.

Now Althusser drew a copy of *Mad Magazine* from his inside pocket and pointed to Alfred E. Neuman. "You cannot mistake the similarity to JFK." Adamant, he slapped it with the backs of his knuckles.

"Where did you get that?"

"This?" He held up the magazine. "From the newsagent. I steal it."

Greenberg didn't think Kennedy looked like Alfred E. Neuman. Maybe a little around the forehead, and the eyelids, but he was a prince compared to that toad Khrushchev. And Kennedy was six feet tall while Khrushchev was five two, and Stalin not much bigger, both a couple of dwarfs, a pair of pig-humping peasants, thick-necked and big-eared and cabbage-breathed, though sly in that Slavic way. Of course Ike, for all his heroics, looked like a shrunken head.

Althusser slotted Mad back in his pocket and gave it a pat.

Mutually Assured Destruction, said Greenberg to himself. It was all supposed to have ended in '45 and yet here they were at it again, different teams, same old game.

Althusser leaned forward, hands on the dashboard, and gazed up at a wedge of Canada geese passing overhead like a squadron of fighter jets. "Formidable." *For-mee-dabluh*.

Each time the Frenchman moved a sour smell was awakened. Perhaps it was the odour of the disease Wittgenstein called philosophy. Had Wittgenstein stunk?

"It shall be the policy of this nation to regard any nuclear missile launched from Cuba against any nation in the Western Hemisphere as an attack by the Soviet Union on the United States, requiring a full retaliatory response upon the Soviet Union."

"Armageddon," said Althusser, savouring the word's Wagnerian music, its bass notes of destruction, its Biblical grandeur.

Greenberg did not want a nuclear strike, no matter how measured. He still had hopes for the future, his future. He hadn't fought in the war, though he'd killed a few reputations, and a goose with a rake handle when he was five, an act that still pained him to recall, especially since the goose had done nothing more than express its gooseness by hissing at him. At the time it seemed an unbearable disapproval.

He swung between envy and disdain for Althusser. Althusser had spent four and a half years in a German POW camp; Greenberg had spent the war battling it out in the lofts and galleries of New York, a campaign no less bloody for its guerrilla nature. Althusser had survived on rotting horse meat; Greenberg had ridden horses in Central Park. Althusser had strangled his wife; Greenberg had penned scathing reviews.

"Now your leaders are no longer Cuban leaders inspired by Cuban ideals. They are puppets and agents of an international conspiracy which has turned Cuba into the first Latin American country to become a target for nuclear war…"

Gripping the steering wheel, Greenberg took the car into a tight curve. It responded as if it had eyes of its own, like a well-trained horse. Mounted at either corner of the hood were two sleek ornaments that looked like missiles while the dashboard was gleaming and curvaceous, the interior red and cream. Again he admired the engineering, the attention to colour and form. Fuck those Germans, this was Yankee work.

"Last night I also dream of my father screaming in his sleep," said Althusser. "He would scream every night like a wolf. He would howl because his soul hurt and I would lie in my bed very frightened. Did I tell you he bought me a rifle when I was nine?"

"No."

"I tried to shoot the sun out of the sky. I missed." This seemed to disappoint him.

Greenberg's father had been too dogged to dream. As for his own dreams, the few he recalled were disappointingly re-alistic, chronologically plotted with rising action and charac-ter growth and denouements, which was why whenever the subject came up—and it came up a lot at cocktail parties lately where everyone seemed to be in analysis—he invented all manner of fantastic imagery. De Quincey dreams, steamy and jungular, rank with the musk of big cats and leering assassins. What he wouldn't do to be visited in his dreams by one of Tit-ian's golden-skinned sluts or an Ingres' Odalisque.

"…medium range nuclear missiles with a range of one thou-sand nautical miles capable of striking Washington DC…"

Althusser had pled insanity to the charge of having stran-gled his wife. As Professor of Philosophy at the École Normale Supérieure in Paris he swung a lot of weight. The directors were more than indulgent and it had become a cause célébre to reclaim such an exalted mind from the abyss. No surprise, really. The same had happened with Genet when they wanted to put him away for life. Sartre, Cocteau, and Picasso had rallied around and got him off.

Greenberg sank into his seat. It was a comfortable seat. He enjoyed the sensation of the world coming to him, of sitting like a king on his throne and watching it approach on its knees. Not that he was a megalomaniac, he was proud, though not without reason. Humbleness, after all, was but a small virtue. Who had said that? Perhaps he had. Then again it was hum-bling, and no small source of bitterness, to think that if he were to strangle someone he couldn't name anyone who'd rally around him.

But then hadn't he always been alone?

He renewed his grip on the wheel. The first stop on their journey would be Niagara Falls, second the Emma Lake artists colony north of Regina, Saskatchewan, where Greenberg was to be critic-in-residence, and finally the mental hospital in Weyburn, back down south near the border, where Althusser was due for psychiatric treatment.

Althusser had insisted on seeing Niagara Falls, for he had his wife's ashes in a vase in the trunk and meant to pour them into the thundering cascade, a gesture he said she would have liked. After the fire of the crematorium, the plunge into the abyss, a plunge that one way or another awaited them all.

Now Kennedy was saying something about bombers that could range as far north as Hudson's Bay and as far south as Lima.

Greenberg jutted his chin toward the radio. "What do you think?"

Althusser blew air scornfully. "It does not matter what I think."

"But you're Althusser."

He shrugged as if suddenly nothing at all mattered, not even himself.

As Greenberg watched the lines tick by, he evaluated that shrug: indifference or weakness? He swallowed drily and, feeling cruel and voyeuristic, asked, "Do you think you could do it again?"

Althusser stared out the passenger-side window at low, rolling hills and a few scattered deciduous trees turning red and orange. "You have seen Them?"

"Who?"

"*Them*. The movie," said Althusser. "Ants bigger than this

car. I like this movie very much. It is something out of Jules Verne. And *Lolita*. I think this one is also very French. Not American at all."

In the distance a factory stack pumped black fists of smoke.

"And the sirens wail like sirens," intoned Althusser. "But I look forward—purely out of scientific interest you understand—to learn what these doctors will say regarding my poor tête."

It seemed to Greenberg that Althusser wasn't as depressed as he should be. Yes, it had been two years since he'd killed his wife, and yes he'd beaten the murder charge, and most importantly perhaps was the fact that the man was on massive medication, six tablets of varying size, shape and colour that morning at breakfast. Jean Claude, his nurse and guard and escort, had been strict in seeing Althusser take them on time and in order. We're molecules, thought Greenberg, and saw the phrase in large looping cursive on a wall in a gallery. Text decontextualized. *This is not a pill.*

"So," Greenberg prompted, "you could...kill again?"

Althusser exhaled long. "I don't know. I was..." His mouth worked as though he was choking and he could only shake his head. "Don't ask. Please." He hung his head, perhaps the first genuine emotion displayed since his arrival in the US.

Greenberg let him alone. He wished the man no more pain than necessary. Fields flew past. How vast the sky was, the clouds tectonic, causing him to think of Constable and envy a life spent studying the sky. Constable and Turner both. He drove on feeling his jowls droop and his shoulders sag.

Then from the corner of his eye he saw Althusser's left hand began to levitate—eerily—and whip down onto the back of his neck like a medieval penitent punishing himself with a knotted rope. He studied a mosquito on his palm.

"I'm sorry," said Greenberg, only partly lying. "It's none of my business. I shouldn't have pried."

"I am what I am. Like Popeye the Sailor man." Althusser wiped his palm on his pant leg then took out his pipe, curved black stem, glossy chestnut bowl, and was soon sucking wetly like an infant at the breast. He exhaled smoke that unfurled in a small mushroom cloud against the windshield. "It is possible that I need a sweat lodge."

But Greenberg wanted this lapsed Catholic's demons alive and well; no exorcisms until after the deadly deed he had in store for him.

"And a haircut as well." Althusser cranked the rearview his way and studied the state of his hair. "Hair is dead, you know. And yet we spend so much time on it. Like morticians."

Greenberg's was all but gone, and what remained had migrated to his ears and ass. He might have lamented this disappearance but he'd never been regarded as handsome so he accepted it. He too was what he was, and took solace in the fact that he was powerful, that he was Greenberg, and that more than a few women—twenty-seven in fact—had given themselves to him, which more than made up for a few strands of dead hair. Or almost.

They passed a sign for Niagara Falls then a town with warehouses and light industry, factory chimneys venting smoke that stretched horizontally like charcoal windsocks.

"We stay there! Turn! Quickly! *Vite*!" Althusser grabbed at the steering wheel but Greenberg fended him off with his elbow. Flying along the highway at sixty miles per hour they fought, Althusser prying at Greenberg's fingers, Greenberg gripping the wheel tighter. The scrawny Frenchman was surprisingly strong.

"Stop it! We'll crash!"

"Turn!"

The motel had a twitching neon waterfall beneath the word *Niagara*.

"We have reservations at the Howard Johnson!"

"You fool! It is the first place Jean Claude will look."

Greenberg saw the logic so swung the Dodge into the lot.

Althusser hunkered low as he spied over the seat and spoke in a gritty voice. "Stash zee car around back."

ॐ

Greenberg checked them in then arranged to meet Althusser in the restaurant in half an hour. They had separate but adjoining rooms. His smelled musty and the beige chenille bedcover was worn nearly transparent. He set his suitcase in a corner, dropped into a low-backed chair of lime green Naugahyde then pried off his Hush Puppies and flexed his toes. Shutting his eyes he took some deep breaths. When he opened them he saw the Rembrandt on the wall. *Self Portrait at the Age of 63*. Even in a warped print under smudged glass the genius was undeniable. There he is, the old bastard, staring at life and death, the past and the future. Is there remorse in his eyes, in the way the lids sit, and in the set of his mouth, as if he's just about to swallow his fear, as if he knows that he only has months to live? And the brow with its hint of a frown and coarse skin. But it's those black eyes that hold you, all the more so when contrasted by the light on his upper forehead and cheeks and the oblivion surrounding him. Sixty-three years old, twelve years older than Greenberg now. Did the great man assume that three hundred years hence someone like Greenberg would sit in a room looking at his picture? Did Rembrandt Harmenszoon van Rijn contemplate the future?

Greenberg lay his hands over his face as if they were a cool cloth and thought of his own future. He needed a plan. You didn't kill a person without a plan unless you were an idiot willing to spend the rest of your life in prison or fry in the chair. This wasn't France, he had no loyal followers much less colleagues who'd rally around him. Once again he tasted bile.

He reached for his suitcase and pressed the latches; they snapped out like brass fangs. On top of his clothes was a copy of *Art International*, and on the cover was his face. Usually his face, for all its homeliness, on a magazine cover was a good thing, but this time his mug was on a canvas mounted on an easel battered by splats of blood-like paint. And to the left stood a guy in a suit who looked like Groucho Marx winding up to hurl yet another hardball of red. The caption: "Red Versus Green: Rosenberg lets fly at Greenberg." No need to open the magazine to page 43 and read the article— three and three-quarter pages long—for it was scored into his heart, burned like a brand that still smoked with the scent of his own charred flesh. *Rosenberg*. Greenberg's guts writhed. He twisted the magazine, spindled it, cranked it until his wrists ached then pressed it flat and stared some more. That Rosenberg grin, that self-satisfaction, forever smirking, per- petually pleased, always about to deliver some punchline, some *bon mot*, the bastard was full of *bon mots*. The maga- zine had a circulation of fifteen hundred, not much but it was influential and widespread, from New York to Chicago to Los Angeles, London, Paris, Rome, and everywhere in between that mattered. Greenberg had already bought and burned dozens of copies.

Rosenbackstabber's most recent assault was to write that Greenberg was, quote: yesterday's news. Art, he said, had moved on. Greenberg was in the past tense—the *permanent* past tense.

Aside from bad poetry, Rosenberg's sole claim to glory was inventing Smokey the Bear. An ad man. A maker of posters. A shill. A lackey. A bum sucker. Who knew, maybe he was behind the tiger tail. It certainly seemed his speed.

Rosenberg was trying to supplant Greenberg by promoting something he'd been calling "Action Painting," insisting that a canvas was an event, not an object but an event. Well, Greenberg had an event planned for him.

Twenty-five years he'd known Rosenberg. Sure, the guy was the better talker, smooth and witty and, he hated to say it, with a winning manner, the gift of the gab, the honeyed tongue, smart guy always making with the jokes. On the page, however, Greenberg could KO him in a paragraph—in a single line. He'd done it before and he'd do it again, because he was Greenberg, the fifties had been his decade, he'd owned it. Pollock had been his discovery even if Rosenberg had known him first, and abstract expressionism was his, Greenberg's, movement. Then along comes Rosen-upstart wanting to take him down. And with what? *Action Painting*? Excuse me? In short: it doesn't matter what's on the canvas, that's a by-product, chaff, detritus, what counts is the process, the act. The question of what you hang in a gallery, of how you judge, view, appreciate, of just what the hell you do with "an act" not even the fork-tongued Rosensnake could answer. Oh, the ludicrosity of it all. It was so clearly false and hollow and specious that Rosenberg should have been scorned out of the amphitheatre, driven from the polis, sent into exile on a Bulgarian mountaintop where vultures would come each day and pluck out his tongue.

Yet here he was thrashing Greenberg on the cover of *Art International*.

Casting about for something to divert himself, he pulled last Sunday's *New York Times* from his suitcase and turned the pages, pausing to scan the comics, Dick Tracy, Rex Morgan M.D., Nancy haranguing Sluggo for being a lout. He found the depictions of Nancy and Sluggo disturbing, half child and half adult, their heads so round, the panel so clean, while at the same time a not altogether uninteresting attention to the vagaries of language. What was this? An interview with that beatnik nutbar Timothy Leary, recently fired from Harvard for advocating LSD. Even more provocatively, he was insisting that the Cuban Missile Crisis could be solved in a single afternoon by having JFK and Khrushchev drop acid together. The experience would teach them that "no amount of weapons, nuclear or otherwise, could bring about world peace." Leary offered to provide the dope and the setting. He claimed to have tried several times to reach Kennedy but had been given the run around by White House flunkies. LSD was what awaited Althusser at the asylum in Saskatchewan.

But not before he did a job, not before he did an encore, for if Althusser could throttle his wife then snapping Rosenberg's neck should be a cakewalk.

Yet how to convince him? Money? Althusser had once been renowned for his cheapness, hoarding centimes, stashing them in walls and under floorboards, picking coins out of the gutter and strolling out of cafés without paying, to which the Parisians responded "Bravo!" But with the war and his time as a POW money had lost its value to him, and he'd become famously indifferent to the stuff.

Tossing the paper aside, Greenberg sank back in the chair and shut his eyes. At such moments, lacking whisky, he sought solace not in the art of Pollock but called up in his memory the work of affable old Raoul Dufy, whose village scenes with their warm colours and quietly contained lives were a reassuring if illusory balm.

❧

He found Althusser chewing a black liquorice cigar and performing surgery on an Aero Bar, sawing it in half with a steak knife to expose the interior architecture of tiny air pockets. Along with the Areo bar he had a Sweet Marie, a Jersey Milk, a Coffee Crisp, a Kit Kat, a Mounds, a Pep Chew, and a Cherry Blossom, all arranged in a row.

Pulling the liquorice cigar from his lips he apologized for the meagre selection. "I bought everything they had. *C'est tout.*"

"You have a sweet tooth."

"Yes, my teeth are sweet."

The waitress appeared with coffee that rolled about the pot like a blob of black mercury. Her uniform was the colour of custard. Late afternoon sun highlighted loose strands of back-combed blonde hair along the curve of her neck. Her teeth were perfect.

"You are very beautiful..." Althusser squinted at her name tag. "Dot."

She'd heard it before. "Sweet tooth, do ya?"

Althusser opened his arms offering her anything from his hoard of chocolate, anything at all.

"You boys going to watch Milhauser?"

For a moment Althusser and Greenberg were at one in their bewilderment. Greenberg asked who Milhauser was.

"He's going over the falls tomorrow in a barrel."

Althusser raised his cup for a refill and said that for all its faults he liked this country very much. "What time do you finish your work, Dot?"

She'd heard this before as well. "What part of France you from?"

"Algeria."

"You serve?"

"POW. Schleswig-Holstein. Four and one half years."

She sucked her perfect teeth and regarded him with new respect. "I was in a camp in Mindanao for two."

⊙╬⊙

Back in his room, an expanse of cold empty bedsheet stretched away on either side of Greenberg. He was lonely. There had been women over the previous few years, but not the one he wanted, Helen, Helen Frankenthaler, young, beautiful, talented, driven, his equal and more. Rolling onto his side he faced the motel sign flashing through the curtain, pulsing and insistent. He rolled the other way and watched the sign throbbing on the wall. He rolled onto his stomach but that hurt his neck, so he ended up on his back once again, staring upward, wishing Helen was here, now, in bed with him.

He must have slept, for he woke to sounds of a struggle that were most definitely coming from Althusser's room. Creeping to the adjoining door, Greenberg put his ear to the cool wood. Bedsprings. A choked voice. Greenberg saw it all: Althusser strangling Dot. Who else could it be? He was horrified, for if Althusser got arrested he wouldn't be able to strangle Rosentoad, which meant he'd have to do it himself. He sagged against the wall. But even in despair his imagination forged on, and a scenario presented itself: *a walk through the Saskatchewan wilderness—they had to have miles of the stuff up there—a long walk, just him and Rosenweasel, all howyadoin' boyo, hows-about we bury the hatchet—then whadaya know he fell and hit his head. One minute we're discussing Barney Newman and the next kaboom he's down, a stroke I thought, or some kinda seizure, smashes his head on a stone, these tall skinny drink-of-water type guys are frail...* Greenberg's mind was so intent on possibilities that when he finally yanked open the door to stop Althusser and save Dot he scarcely knew what he was seeing—like the first time he saw a Pollock (oh, holy moment)—a painting yes, but so new. This, before him, was a strangling, yes, but Dot was on top, with her hands around Althusser's throat, and Althusser in a choked voice was urging her to squeeze harder…

Tuesday, 23 October, 1962

They rendezvoused in the restaurant the following morning at eight. A beaming Althusser sat behind an array of meat: back bacon, two types of sausage, ham and eggs, some sort of cutlet. He stabbed a piece of steak and offered a tally-ho as Greenberg slid into the booth. Althusser was shaved bald.

"You got a haircut."

"Dot used my razor."

"Where is Dot?"

"AA meeting."

"She did a good job," said Greenberg, admiring the sleekness of his scalp. There was not a nick in sight. It took years off him.

"Yes, I am very pleased." He caressed his skull then attacked his steak again. "There were no eels on the menu. Do you like eels?"

Greenberg and Helen had eaten eels in Paris. They'd also found flies in a bottle of wine and, so in love at the time, so irrepressibly buoyant, so unabashedly goofy and innocent and willing to indulge a bad pun, they'd laughed saying the wine was full-bodied, and went ahead and drank it anyway. Seven years later and he still missed her.

A waitress most definitely not Dot arrived dangling a Pyrex pot of coffee from one finger. She had several pencils stabbed at angles through her beehive.

"Do you have danish?" asked Greenberg.

"Prune."

"Fine. Good. And some of that." He pointed to the coffee and she tilted the tar-like brew into his cup.

A New York Times was open at Althusser's elbow, folded lengthwise so as not to impinge upon his feast.

Greenberg read the headline upside down: "Soviet Challenges US Right to Blockade".

Althusser dialled the paper for Greenberg's benefit. He read, *Insisting that the weapons provided by the Soviet Union were designed solely for enhancing Cuba's defence potential, the Soviet statement asserted the United States demands that military equipment Cuba needs for self-defence should be removed from Cuban territory, a demand which naturally no state which values its independence can meet...*

Althusser forked up an entire fried egg and folded it into his mouth.

"Twenty-five ships en route to Cuba," said Greenberg with foreboding.

"All loaded with nuclear warheads," said Althusser with joy. His grin caused yolk to seep from the corners of his mouth.

"This is bad."

"The Fates are terrible," observed the Frenchman, dabbing his mouth with his serviette.

"You believe in fate?"

"I believe in science. But there is fortune as well. Only a fool would deny this. It is fortunate to be here, now, in this place." He gazed at the ceiling as if to bask in the life-giving rain of bombs that was about to start falling.

"This is hardly ground zero."

"It does not matter, my friend. When the flash comes we will see each others' bones." He sawed jauntily into a pork chop. "They are truly blind, those bitches."

Greenberg tried remembering the names of the Fates: Clotho the Spinner, Lachesis the Apportioner, and the third, the one who cut the thread of your life, what was her name? "I'd rather be in France."

Althusser was appalled. "*Mais non!*"

"Or New Zealand, or Chile, as far from here as possible."

"To be here now makes me alive." Althusser grew rapturous. "The Titans are flexing their muscles."

Or Java, thought Greenberg, somewhere slow and tropical, somewhere out of the trade winds bearing their cargo of radiation. Too bad Rosenberg wasn't in Washington where a bomb would reduce him to a glowing tumour.

"Yes," sang Althusser, "Dot and I will be in each other's arms, enjoying *la petit mort* in the middle of Zee Big One."

Atropos the Inevitable. The cutter of the thread.

❦

As Greenberg and Althusser stepped from the taxi they felt the vibration of the falls, the pavement trembling with a subterranean palsy. A vibrumble, thought Greenberg pleased with the neologism. There were few things he enjoyed more than coining a new word. He inhaled the chill mist. Fragments of rainbow hung like cathedral glass arrested in mid-collapse.

"The vaults of Hades," crooned Althusser. He checked his wig and rearranged his breasts. Greenberg had advised a pantsuit, or pedal pushers, but Althusser had fallen in love with a pleated cotton skirt that fell to mid-shin. It was yellow with blue flowers, too spring-timey for the season but Althusser would not be dissuaded. He was a Parisian; what was Greenberg but an American? The wig was long and straight and blonde, the blouse white and ruffled over the bosom. The brassiere was given authentic heft by party balloons filled with milk. He wore a sweater of lilac cashmere, with bone buttons, cape-like over his thin shoulders. The ensemble was completed by cerise lipstick and horned sunglasses and a scarf—grey with a fringe of purple beads—prudently looped about his neck to hide the bruising on his Adam's apple from Dot's thumbs.

Althusser had been surprisingly eager to ditch Jean Claude. And he'd warned that he'd be on their tails so they must take extra precautions, which was how Greenberg found himself wearing a golf hat and a Jerry Colonna moustache, black and heavy and waxed, smelling of contact cement. If that's what it took to separate the two Frenchman and get Althusser under his control, it was a small sacrifice. Taking a cab instead of the Dodge was the final precaution. The urn containing the ashes was in the straw beach bag over Althusser's forearm.

Greenberg had wanted to miss the falls entirely. In this one thing he and Jean Claude had been in agreement. Yet Althusser had insisted, eyes growing dim and narrow and his head withdrawing tortoise-like into his shoulders in defiance of opposition. A man who could argue Sartre, de Beauvoir, and Lacan under the table all in a single evening while Beckett looked on in bemusement.

Now Althusser gripped the iron railing and leaned as far over the water as he could stretch, the better to embrace the full experience of height and roar and mist. He was shouting, "This is the way I want to die!"

"What if you live?"

"Then I am a god!" cried Althusser. "Have you been to Jerusalem? You must go to Jerusalem."

Greenberg had not been to Jerusalem. Israel didn't interest him. Although he had spent his childhood speaking Yiddish he no longer felt particularly Jewish, and perhaps never really had. The aesthetics had always bored and depressed him, the gabardine, the elflocks, no paintings in the synagogue. Maybe he was a closet Catholic? Say what you would, the bastards could paint. What he had felt was that he was an outsider, a stranger, a feeling that continued into adulthood to this very day. Gripping the wet cold iron railing he gazed down into the cascading whitewater and thought of Hiroshima, shattered atoms spinning like blown motes. "Jerusalem? Why?"

"Because it is the home of three gods." He rubbed his hands together. "I should have bought the gloves." He had admired a pair of sleek elbow-length gloves of pearly silk and then settled for red nail polish. His hands resembled chicken's feet dipped in blood.

It seemed to Greenberg that these falls were a place of apocalypse, and yet looking around he saw happy faces. On this Tuesday afternoon in the land of hot dogs and Coca Cola no one was worried. The World Series had ended only last week, the hockey, football and basketball seasons were hitting stride, Halloween was coming up and Father Knew Best.

He and Helen had come here once on a lark, a folly, a whim, a madcap romp intended to be ironic and sardonic and wry; in the spirit of Walter Benjamin they would be cultural spies on-the-slum. How many beautiful, talented young women could he do that with?

Now he gazed at the people enjoying the falls. Perhaps it was a last act of innocence, a way to shield their children's eyes from the horror. They yipped and laughed, parents and grandparents, gangs of kids, young couples with toddlers on leashes as though they were a species of pet. A little girl in pink pressed her palms over her ears and shrieked. Greenberg thought of Munch.

Althusser's skirt billowed on the updraft and in an act of becoming modesty he pressed it down then pointed to the far side of the falls. "What is over there?"

"I don't know," said Greenberg. "Canada. Toronto."

"The Lone Ranger's faithful companion."

Greenberg wondered when Milhauser was supposed to go over. He recalled something about a black man named Nathan Boya going over last summer in a sphere of rubber-lined sheet metal and coming out with a concussion and broken collar bone but otherwise smiling.

"Kiss me you fool."

Althusser caught Greenberg's face between his hands and clamped his mouth to his. To Greenberg's horror he found himself aroused. He gripped Althusser's shoulders and held him at arm's length though did not let go, his mind already two moves ahead; if a little intimacy would facilitate the murder of Rosenberg then so be it.

"Hug me."

Greenberg hugged him.

Althusser whispered wetly in his ear, "Jean Claude is here. Now, put your arm around me and walk this way."

They strolled off alongside the railing. Engrossed with the spectacle of the falls, no one paid any attention to the homely couple. A breeze gusted up bearing the fresh mulchy scent of leaves and mist. A young girl angled an umbrella trying to catch the wind and shouting, "Mary Poppins!"

Up ahead a man on an upended whisky barrel addressed a crowd.

"It is Milhauser!" Althusser began to run with surprising agility on his high heels.

Greenberg followed. Milhauser turned out to be a monkey in a tailored space suit, the stars and stripes on the chest. His handler, a dwarf called Sylvester, announced that this would be Milhauser's third voyage over the falls. Sylvester screwed the helmet over the monkey's head then opened the top of the barrel and shoved the monkey in followed by a hand of bananas. Donations were being accepted in a Folgers coffee can. Sylvester selected four children, two girls and two boys, to roll the barrel to the gap in the rail serving as the launch pad.

"God speed!" called Sylvester through a megaphone, then led the crowd in a countdown. At one the kids rolled the barrel off the edge. When it hit the river the current snatched it away sucking it toward the foaming falls where it plunged, spinning, down and down, then vanished. Greenberg found himself swallowing bile as if he himself was in the spinning barrel, vomiting and shitting amid the mashed bananas. He turned away. And found himself face-to-face with Jean Claude. On his foot was a fresh white cast covered in a clear plastic bag.

Greenberg said, "It was an accident."

Jean Claude said, "This is not." He stripped the fake moustache from Greenberg's upper lip then stomped Greenberg's toe, sending him pogo-sticking down the pathway clutching his foot.

"There are no accidents," observed Althusser.

Jean Claude said, "The car waits."

"You found it."

"I find it, I find you. Your business here is complete?"

Althusser halted, horrified at what he'd nearly forgotten. He pulled the ceramic urn with its Oriental dragon out of his woven bag and returned to the railing where he unscrewed the cap, raised the urn high in both hands and with great and solemn ceremony kissed it then poured the ashes. They slid out like a grey scarf drawn by an invisible hand to vanish over the water.

ৎ৾ঌ

Jean Claude consulted the map and decided it would be faster to cross into Canada and skirt the northern shores of Lakes Huron and Michigan then cut back into the States and travel along the southern edge of Lake Superior. The customs official on the Canadian side of the Falls looked at Althusser's passport, leaned to look at Althusser's face, then looked again at the passport.

"He is an actor," said Jean Claude.

The official took this in, nodding in the skeptical manner of his profession. "What's he been in?"

Jean Claude looked at Althusser as though expecting him to recite his filmography.

Greenberg said, "*Blood and Roses*."

"Yes," said Jean Claude. "*Blood and Roses*."

"*Blood and Roses*," said the customs man.

"It was about vampires," explained Greenberg.

Baring his teeth and hissing, Althusser raised his hands and wiggled his red-nailed fingers with menace.

The man considered this. His face was a pale grey beneath his peaked white cap with its maple leaf badge. It was late in the afternoon and his five o'clock shadow was coming on strong. Scratching his belly beneath his dark blue shirt he compressed his thin lips and exhaled out his narrow nose. He dealt with a lot of Quebecers but not so many French French. There were some famous French French actors, like Charles Boyer, Jean Gabin, Belmondo, and that Maurice Chevalier from *Gigi*. He didn't much like musicals—too much singing— nor did he like that Chevalier had been a commie. This one here might be a homo. His Uncle Chet had been a big one for the lady's clothes, though that had been for amateur theatre. He'd played Desdemona and got kissed by a black man, not a real black man but Del Rogerson in blackface. Uncle Chet drank white wine instead of beer, and they called him Begonia because of all the cologne he wore even though Chet pointed out that begonias didn't have a scent. But Chet was a good guy, his dad's brother—he'd looked just like him, same voice, same build, same hair—and had given him a hockey stick for his ninth birthday.

Stepping back the man waved them through. "Proceed."

⁖

A mile out of Sudbury they rolled up the windows against the stench of sulphur and rotten eggs. The setting sun gilded the scrolling smoke while ranks of enraged crows racketed from wires.

"The welcoming committee," said Althusser who raised his right hand and twirled it like the Queen.

The darkly carpeted Trencherman Arms had axes crisscrossed over shields on the trowelled walls, while suits of armour stood guard on either side of the TV where the announcer delivered a brooding update on the missile crisis.

Althusser ignored the screen and busied himself with removing his wig, combing it with a dessert fork and setting it at one end of the table. He asked the waitress if they had red wine.

The waitress was all of nineteen and eager to please. Her high and pointy bosom suggested twin nuclear warheads, the puff sleeves of her blouse roiling mushroom clouds; her blond hair coiled at either ear like vortices of white smoke. She said yes indeed they most certainly did have red wine.

"What kind?"

She was confused. "Red."

"Bordeaux?"

Her gazed flickered around for help. "Just, I don't know, red."

Althusser was not without empathy. He smiled. "Then bring us a bottle eh, bebe!" And he began furiously scratching his scalp with all ten fingers.

"You should change," said Jean Claude.

"I have changed," stated Althusser. "I am a new man in the New World. Context. It is all!"

Greenberg's swollen toe was throbbing, his upper lip stung, and he needed an Aspirin, he needed a dozen Aspirin, a whole bottle. Where was that wine?

Jean Claude wore a black, wool turtleneck with the long sleeves pushed up revealing hirsute and sinewy forearms. He was about the same age as Althusser and had the same long narrow nose that made Greenberg shudder at the fragility of gristle and bone. He wondered if they could possibly be related, both had been born in Algeria, both were gaunt and grey-eyed, though Jean Claude was taller and fitter, the son who would have been favoured by the father, the rugged athlete compared to the frail, cerebral and decidedly odd Louis.

They had the restaurant to themselves. Raw log posts, wrought iron sconces, an abundance of wood and leather and iron, a low odour of carpet and soup. When the wine arrived Althusser poured, held his glass high to judge the colour, brought it to his nose to test the bouquet, winked at Greenberg and Jean Claude, said "Salut," and then sipped. "Shoe leather and motor oil. Bon. In the camp we boiled dandelions and nails and were content."

They all ordered baron of beef.

Greenberg asked the waitress for a double Scotch and also if she might turn the TV to the American news.

Standing on her toes—a not unfetching posture, one that Degas might have sketched—she switched stations, dial ratcheting loudly at each turn, until she found the stalwart Walter Cronkite, with his voice of reason, his eyebrows of wisdom, his moustache of masculinity, patriarch, pillar, bearer of tidings, more reliable than the president himself; Greenberg had always been sceptical of the Kennedy mythos, suspecting the endemic frailties of the inbred.

"The world is on edge this evening. The blockade appears
—*appears*—to be working. Early unconfirmed reports state
that Soviet ships are changing course away from Cuba. But
the president is grave and he is cautious. For still other reports
suggest that some ships, escorted by nuclear submarines, are
staying the course and continuing on into the Caribbean Sea.
U-2 reconnaissance sorties report three R-12 missile sites on
Cuba. These rockets have the range to hit Washington and
New York. And each of these three sites has a stockpile esti-
mated at eight megatons, more than all the explosives ever
utilized in the entire history of war. Add to this Fidel Castro's
arsenal of SAMs—surface-to-air missiles—as well as his army
of three hundred thousand and we have the potential for
holocaust."

The grimmest word in the English language. And yet when
Walter said it with that calm sobriety, that besuited manliness,
that aura of absolute control, it was impossible not to be
reassured that right would prevail, and what nation was more
right than America? Greenberg envisioned Cronkite finishing
up his evening broadcast and repairing to his favourite bar, a
darkly gleaming wood-grained redoubt with a hushed mood
and muted jazz, to savour a single malt and a cigarette and
shake his head at all the fuss.

Greenberg signalled for another Scotch.

Althusser soaked his serviette in his ice water and draped
it across his itchy scalp.

Jean Claude dipped his baron of beef and stared at the
screen. "These sister fuckers, they will blow us to shit."

"We will live underground," said Althusser as if the prospect
was pleasing, "in the coal mines. Zola will laugh in his grave.
We will become moles, our eyes blind, our skins pale, tunnelling
through the dirt with our long fingers." He raised his hands and
wriggled his digits as though he was not merely ready but eager.

"You're sick in the head," said Greenberg.

"Of course. That is why you are taking me to the hospital. They will give me drugs. New drugs. LSD. Do you know LSD? No? They say it is the Golden Door. Foucault takes it all the time and he is much improved. Chemistry, my friends, we are molecules, protons and electrons and neutrons. Nuclear bombs waiting to explode." He mimed an elegant blast with his spidery fingers.

Greenberg set his elbows on the table and leaned his head into his hands. Althusser was toying with him. Nothing enraged Greenberg more than not being taken seriously. All his life he'd been driven by that goal, to be read, studied, quoted as an authority—*the* authority, and this mad Frenchman was playing him for a fool.

"You have seen this movie *The Fly*? That is us. Stuck. In a web."

Greenberg couldn't bear any more. "But you're the one who believes in forging the new man!"

Althusser cackled: "Alfred E. New Man. Please, do not give me the second rate ravings of left wing humanism. I am a scientist. I believe in the science of society, of revolution. If you had read my books you would know this."

"How many of *my* books have *you* read?"

"You have written books?" Althusser frowned, bewildered.

Greenberg nearly choked.

Jean Claude actually smiled.

Althusser said, "I do not read—I think."

Greenberg slapped the table causing the cups to bounce in their saucers.

"Greenbairg," growled Jean Claude, "you know nothing."

"Ah, but he is an expert on art and culture," chirped Althusser.

"Whose art? Whose culture?"

"Excellent questions, my friend," agreed Althusser.

The frogs were ganging up on him. Greenberg imagined punching Jean Claude's face, breaking that beak of a nose, bursting that sullen lower lip, bending all those yellow teeth. He'd slugged a few people in his time, hauled off and popped them at cocktail parties and galleries, not that he was proud of it, but some schmo who hadn't even heard of Kant or Santayana starts pronouncing and it damn well behoved you to biff the bugger. But Jean Claude was smiling a smile that was a little too confident. Greenberg crossed his arms over his chest and clamped his fists in his armpits to restrain himself.

Pushing his plate away, Jean Claude sucked his teeth with distaste then checked his wristwatch. "It is late. We have twelve hundred and fifty miles to Weyburn. We can do it in three days. You," he said to Greenberg, "you can fuck off. Come, go, I don't give two squirts of goose shit. After Weyburn, I don't want to see you again. Ever." *Ayvair*. He gestured as though Greenberg was no better than the rotten egg stench of the Sudbury air. He stood. "We go to the room."

Althusser pouted though seemed to enjoy Jean Claude's assertiveness. He picked up his wig and positioned it on his head while Jean Claude did his best to walk with a casual grace in spite of the white cast weighting the end of his leg.

When they were gone, Greenberg signalled the waitress for another double. Dobie Gillis came on the TV. There was Dwayne Hickman seated at the base of Rodin's *The Thinker* in a pose of intense, if not exactly profound, cogitation. It was the sort of thing Pop artists—if you could call sophomoric pranksters like Warhol artists—would celebrate. And yet, here was a great sculpture on display to the masses. Perhaps it was possible to elevate this middle class that was expanding year by year; today Dobie Gillis, tomorrow *Macbeth*, and all on the back of capitalism. Someday he would reflect upon this week in history and turn it into a novel. He'd use a pseudo-nym: Clem Bergman, or better yet Greg Melman, or no, Bud Gregory.

Finishing his drink he ordered another. He'd smoked hash and opium and swallowed every pill on the market, but give him Scotch. When it arrived he held it in his hand and admired the glass, weighty, with a scalloped pattern around the base. One good thump with this baby and he could lay Jean Claude out cold. He sipped then gulped. Standing, he winced at the pain in his toe and then limped across the knights and chargers in the carpet and on up the stairs to his room. Once inside, he took stock of his pills: seven Tuinals. He arranged them on the side table, put them in one long row, then in two sets of three with one left over, then in three sets of two with one left over. Look at that solitary fellow, he said to himself. He looks lonely. "Are you lonely?" he asked it. He picked it up and held it in the palm of his hand. "Yes, you're lonely." He tossed it into his mouth and swallowed it down without water. Then, before he could talk himself out of it, he banged back another pill, then lay on the bed wishing he'd ordered one last double, or bought a whole bottle. He pulled his Hush Puppies back on and went along the musty corridor and down the stairs but the restaurant was closed.

❦

The therapist cautioned him.

Clement, only a fool or a man in love keeps his hand in the fire.

She said—

Of course she did—

And I—

Naturally.

And we—

There is strength in solitude, Clement.

I'm talking about my heart.

Clement, you make yourself vulnerable.

I'm human.

Take your hand from the fire.

Helen betrayed me.

Betrayal is natural.

I tell you, we were in love!

Love dies the death of the flower.

I'm too trusting.

Trust is freeing.

Then why do I feel imprisoned?

You are on the Cross.

The Cross?

Money and sex and power, Clement. The trinity.

I have bad thoughts.

Of course you do.

I have thoughts of plunging a knife into Rosenberg's chest and strangling Helen.

This is good. Now we're getting somewhere.

⚜

It did not escape Greenberg that he and Althusser both loved women named Helen. It put them in good company, not only with each other but with antiquity. Yet Greenberg had resisted the urge to kill his Helen when she dumped him. Was this a sign of weakness or wisdom? Was he a male undone by the castration of culture?

He and Helen had spent a couple of afternoons with Althusser and Hélène in Montparnasse in '55. They'd gone to the Jeu de Paume and the Musée National d'art Moderne.

Althusser was dazzled by Klimt and haunted by Ensor. Greenberg cautiously approved of Leger and Villon. They all four took wry delight in looking at Dufy's *Avenue of the Bois du Bologne* and then later in actually walking along the Avenue of the Bois du Bologne and speculating upon which one was the more real. They sat in a café and studied the parade of Parisians. Greenberg, feeling whimsical, a rare experience, had imagined the four of them painted by Velázquez in court finery, ruffs and silks and pearls and wigs, knobbed canes, buckled shoes, scarlet ribbons around their knees, whippets at their feet. With the exception of Helen, they would not have been miscast in the role of inbred royalty, flat-chested, humpbacked, narrow-shouldered cretins, big-nosed and weak-chinned.

The similarity between Helen and Hélène ended at their names. Helen Frankenthaler was more than gorgeous; she was magnetic. French men and women alike strained their necks to look at her and both made remarks catty, envious, and provocative. Hélène Rytman was drawn, gaunt, and stringy, her eyes veined and frantic, her chest flat, hair hopeless. Althusser was equally homely, sad-eyed and sour-mouthed, with a nose like a shard of slate. As for Greenberg, he was bald and bug-eyed, and had a nose that invited the word *schnoz*. Worse, he was getting boobs. Forty-six and his chest wobbled and his belly pudged and his feet were flat and his chest was bad and his gas lethal.

Althusser had lost so much calcium in the war that his bones were brittle and his spine curved, his teeth grey and his fingernails yellowed and flaking. His will however was undiminished and he remained loyal to the Marxist cause in spite of Stalin's tyranny, the systematic starvation of millions of Ukrainians, the horrors of the gulag. When Greenberg mentioned the undeniable American economic boom—wryly adding that this' was clear proof of God's favour—Althusser had pointed to the black writers and musicians fleeing to Paris as evidence of a system that was already in rot.

"And France is so ideal?" Greenberg had demanded. "What about Algeria?"

"Do not talk to me about Algeria," Althusser had said. "It is being handled very badly. It is tragic. But we are pulling out of Indochine even as you fools are going in."

Helen had put her hand on Greenberg's thigh to calm him, but he was too agitated, the fight was on—he could never resist a fight—and he said, "Marx's trial and error has been reduced to Stalin's trial and terror."

Althusser had applauded the pun then reminded him that Stalin was two years in the ground and that Khrushchev was denouncing him daily.

"So you're saying it's a socialist renaissance?"

"We will see. Will you drink absinthe?"

"I'll drink anything."

"Excellent. Still a man of the people in some things."

Greenberg loathed the people and popular culture in every degraded form they took, but he'd had no wish to sour a pleasant day in Paris with a soaring star like Louis Althusser. "In my heart of hearts, if nowhere else."

"Then we drink to the most overrated organ," Althusser had said.

They poured water through sugar into their drinks then gulped and set their glasses down hard.

"I saw your protege Pollock's paintings in what was it? 19 and 52."

Greenberg sought Helen's hand under the table as he awaited Althusser's scorn.

"Interesting," allowed Louis. "But I fear he is but a howl in the storm. The individual is an object of science. The artist is only free inasmuch as he makes us see the lived experience of capitalist society in a critical form. It must throw into relief the dominant categories of ideology as these function to obfuscate history. Does your Pollock do this?"

Greenberg stammered, "Utilitarian art is nothing but political rhetoric."

Althusser blew air scornfully.

Greenberg endeavoured to trace the lineage from Impressionism through Cubism to Abstract Expressionism but within seconds Althusser's eyes had closed, his head had fallen back and he'd begun to snore.

Later, they went to Althusser's apartment where Greenberg and Helen had both been surprised to see a large birdcage with half a dozen canaries singing. Helen had laughed in delight while Hélène had merely smiled thinly, doubtfully, perhaps haunted by the fact that she could love anyone who would cage birds.

Seven years later Greenberg wondered how the canaries had sounded on the sunny spring morning when Althusser pushed his wife down into the bed and pressed his thumbs into her throat.

๑❦๑

The hands on the clock radio drooped like a moustache. Four-forty a.m. Greenberg's head pounded and his toe throbbed. Limping into the bathroom he drank from the faucet. The water tasted of sulphur but he kept drinking, then held his head under the tap until his skull was numb. He tried returning to bed but it was futile; he knew what he was going to do and that there was no way to avoid it. Crossing the room to his suitcase he pulled out the copy of *Art International* and, like a self-mutilator giving in to a bout of scratching, dropped into the armchair and switched on the lamp and stared at the article, just to keep the wounds raw and livid, just to keep the agony fresh and pulsing, just to keep his drive for revenge keen.

"While the action painters set forth onto the white expanse of the canvas like Ishmael onto the expanse of the unknown sea to do battle with the leviathan, Clem Greenberg is content to sit childlike on the shore making sandcastles…"

"Greenberg sounds more like a mouthpiece for government cultural programs than an explicator of the avant-garde."

"More and more from Greenberg we hear less and less of substance, and the result is hot air."

Sandcastles. Government programs. Hot air. Each was a stab in the back. He very nearly whimpered. As much as he loved battle, as much as he enjoyed standing Patton-like upon the smoking field of criticism, as much as the *Sturm und Drang* electrified his spine, such attacks went straight to his heart. The corners of his mouth turned downward and his lower lip quivered.

But the magazine article was not all. It was not the half of it. There was worse. Rosenberg had muscled in on Greenberg's gig at Emma Lake. They'd approached Greenberg first, way back in May, with the invitation to be critic-in-residence, to do a lecture and lead a seminar, all expenses paid, a handsome stipend, a feature interview in *Canadian Art*. Fine. Good. What excellent judgement they were showing, those Canucks. Then a week ago he gets a call saying they want to make it a two-man affair, the thinking being, so it was explained over the static-furred line—didn't these Canadians have proper telephones, were they not in the twentieth century?—to capitalize on the ongoing critical debate between two such esteemed luminaries. "It would be instructive to have divergent opinions. See the heavyweights square off."

They'd even suggested that he and Rosenberg might want to drive up together. Greenberg had nearly ripped the phone out of the wall. And this was all due to start Monday, five days from now.

He checked his watch: pushing five-thirty in the morning and he was already tempted to swallow a couple more Tuinals. He took them out of his shaving kit and gazed upon them as though they were magic beans. What a sweet thing was oblivion. There was no dishonour. It had a fine pedigree going back to Coleridge and De Quincey.

A tap at the door. "Greenbairg... Greenbairg!"

Opening up, Greenberg found Althusser in red silk pyjamas and a ski toque with a maple leaf. "Jean Claude wants to give you the slip. He says you are a bad influence. Are you a bad influence, Greenbairg?" Louis gazed wonderingly, imploringly at him.

Greenberg tried to look innocent.

"I will delay him as much as I can," said Althusser. "But he is eager for an early start."

"I'll be right out."

"It is important that we stay together. The three of us. The Musketeers. Three is a very stable number. Consider the three-legged table. It can stand on any ground."

"Okay."

"Montaigne wrote about the number three."

"I got it," said Greenberg.

"Or was it five?"

"I'll be out in a minute."

"I must reread the essay," muttered Althusser, returning to his room.

Greenberg glanced up and down the musty, carpeted corridor, then shut the door. Discovering the Tuinals still in his hand he shoved them into his coat pocket.

Wednesday, 24 October, 1962

Greenberg found Althusser and Jean Claude at the same table as the night before. The foot with the cast was sticking out at an angle as though Jean Claude wanted everyone to see how he suffered. Greenberg's foot hurt too. He put on a limp, hoping to allay Jean Claude's desire to hurt him further. The guy didn't notice. Nor did Althusser, who was busy loading a slice of toast with egg, positioning it just so, then bearing it on a fork—tines downward—into his mouth. A platter of fried eggs sat in the middle of the table along with a mound of bacon strips glistening under the cartwheel lamp. There was a jug of orange juice, a bowl of apples, pats of butter, a plate of powdered donuts. Greenberg had black coffee and tried not to watch Althusser gorge. The man was insatiable, the food reduced to some sort of pure and volatile fuel.

The TV was off and the doors to the dark wooden cabinet shut. The radio, however, was on and a deep male voice spoke of the tanker *Bucharest* that had been allowed—to the consternation of Nixon and Goldwater—through the American blockade and was proceeding on to Havana, a boarding party having confirmed that it was carrying only fuel oil. The freighter *Marcula*, on the other hand, was proving troublesome. The US Navy was now positioning itself to intercept it, an emergency meeting of the UN National Security Council scheduled for later this afternoon would be televised. Adlai Stevenson and the president were meeting at this very moment, while Khrushchev, the devious little goblin, could not be reached. The Soviet ambassador had filed an official complaint. A dozen years of agreeing to disagree was about to collapse.

Althusser was back in his own clothes. Ignoring the radio, he was chortling over some spoof on Sergeant Bilko in *MAD Magazine* as he ate. Greenberg leaned to see. The caricatures of Phil Silvers displayed undeniable dash, though he rated cartooning a minor genre, limited and adolescent, Cruikshank, Daumier, Beardsley, and Beerbohm notwithstanding. Yet here was the eminent Althusser snickering. The cranky and contradictory French had produced Rabelais and Voltaire and yet loved Jerry Lewis and *MAD*.

By seven they were on the road, Jean Claude at the wheel, Althusser next to him, Greenberg in the rear. They reached Sault Ste. Marie at noon, made a brief stop for gas and sandwiches, and Greenberg managed to purchase a fifth of Ballantine's and fill his flask. They crossed the border back into the States. As they entered Hiawatha National Forest they were greeted by a billboard showing Smokey Bear gripping a shovel like a rifle in one hand and pointing an accusing finger: Only You Can Prevent Forest Fires.

"It is Uncle Sam," said Althusser.

It was Rosenberg. Greenberg would have liked to set it on fire.

Lake Superior stretched away to their right. Depending upon the clouds and the wind it was blue then grey, stippled then smooth, glassy then matte.

A two or three day drive. Greenberg tried to think of a way to get rid of Jean Claude and head directly to Emma Lake and deal with Rosenbastard. By then maybe Althusser wouldn't need the Weyburn Hospital and the LSD, maybe another murder—like another knock on the head—would bring him back to his senses, or whatever passed for them.

Last week Helen had said he was the one who needed a knock on the head. She'd heard of his little trip with Althusser so had phoned, saying, "Clem, you can't be serious."

He was standing in his living room in his underpants, Scotch in one hand, cigarette on his lip, looking in horror at the bulging silhouette of his belly on the wall and trying to reassure himself that in some cultures this was a sign of power and very appealing to women. "Whyever not?"

"One: he's a murderer. Two: he's insane. Three: he has that smell."

"The smell isn't so bad anymore," he lied.

"And he's going where? Some hospital? In *Canada*?"

"Some new treatment they got going."

"*Canada* . . . I mean, what do they *do* up there?"

Greenberg couldn't honestly say. He asked if she was doing any painting?

"Don't ask. What's with Harry? Guy's got a burr up his nose about you."

"That's his moustache."

"Seriously."

"Don't ask. How's Bob?"

She made a noise that meant something along the lines of the honeymoon was over and the hard slog underway and maybe she'd made a mistake and maybe she hadn't.

He allowed himself to be encouraged. He did not wish her misery, but her marriage to Robert Motherwell had crushed him, all the more so since they'd become the golden couple of the New York City art world, which was the only world that counted other than that of Paris.

"Do you remember Paris?" she asked, wistful.

"Of course." He wondered if she was drunk and if she was alone, maybe in bed. He slid his hand into his shorts tempted to have a little pet at the pony then caught himself and loudly cleared his throat, set his drink down and found his pants and, dancing first on one leg then on the other, managed to pull them on even as he continued the conversation. He reached to straighten his tie but wasn't wearing one. He smoothed his hair or what was left of it. She hadn't minded his bald skull...so she'd said. Over the last few years their meetings had been awkward; now she sounded maudlin, and he wondered, perhaps uncharitably, if she needed a favour, for she was an ambitious girl, Helen, not that he blamed her, and of course he'd do anything he could.

"Clem, just be careful, okay."

He knew the tone of voice and was touched, though didn't dare hope she missed him, but of course that was exactly what he did. "What, you've had a premonition?"

"No. I don't know. I don't get them anymore. Not since the meds."

"What are you taking?"

"Oh, pink ones, blue ones. You?"

"Liquid diet," he said.

"We should have smoked opium together."

This intrigued him. They'd read Nerval and Baudelaire and Gautier to each other, but had never taken the next logical step and smoked opium. Would that have made the difference? "You think?"

"I don't know. I'm sorry. I shouldn't have called."

"No, no!"

He paced the apartment wanting to tell her how much he missed her and hated her and missed her and was sorry and oh, by the way, missed her, and if she came right over he'd give her anything, blow off Althusser and Emma Lake and they could get on a plane or boat or hot air balloon back to Paris right now, this very night.

"Look," she said, suddenly sober and brisk, "I just wanted to call and say take care."

❦

The flat tire came on gradually. Greenberg felt it under him, a vague, seasickish sensation, the right rear wheel changing its sound, whirr descending to groan, then the back end of the car slewing on a turn causing Jean Claude to wrestle the wheel, and finally there was the hum of the rim running on a ribbed skin of deflated rubber.

They stood on the side of the road. To the left and right stretched empty highway walled on either side by forest. Jean Claude finished his cigarette and threw it down, then limped to the trunk and heaved out the spare tire, a dull, black pungent disc. Greenberg found its odour curiously appealing, like gasoline or lighter fluid or sulphur. A tire iron clanged down and then a jack. On his knees, Jean Claude wrestled the jack into position, then swore and stood and slapped at the dirt staining his tan trousers. Glaring at Greenberg, he limped to the passenger side and hauled out the floor mat and, using it as a knee pad, resumed cranking the car up. Greenberg felt worse than useless, he felt unmanly, for he'd never changed a tire in his life. He took a step closer thinking he might help, but Jean Claude pointedly ignored him so he settled on an appearance of deference and concern, which involved hovering at a discreet distance ready to pitch in but not getting in the way. No, he and Jean Claude had been at odds from the moment they met, each suspicious of the other. Did Jean Claude have some scheme of his own up his sleeve?

When the wheel was free of the ground, Jean Claude rotated it until he found a shard of Coke bottle embedded deep in the tread. He pried off the hubcap and went to work on the lug nuts, bearing down with his full weight. Each resisted, then gave way with a dry squawk. Now the odours were of iron and grease. Greenberg looked upon the world of the exposed wheel housing, brake, shock, mud flap. The engineering process unfolded in his mind's eye. Design. Foundry.

Manufacture. Parts of steel and parts of plastic. Sheet metal. Zinc. Paint. Glass. Upholstery. The assembly line. He saw it as if in a film scored to the *Carmina Burana*, the glory of industry, Prometheus plasticator, Henry Ford barking orders, then the showroom with its tinted lighting, the besuited sales-man grinning at the eager buyer who gets in behind the wheel and, finally, the open road leading, of course, to some happy future, an American future, the only one worth desiring.

Jean Claude hoisted the spare onto its housing, aligned the holes over the bolts then fit the lug nuts and tightened them by hand and then gave each a single turn with the iron, cinching them slowly, evenly, in series, until they were all snug. Finally the hubcap. He was tense and sweating when he stood. He slapped his hands and then stared in rage at his blackened palms. Greenberg put the wheel into the bottom of the trunk then fetched his flask and took a quick swig. He offered it to Jean Claude, who glared then chugged the entire thing, though not before pouring some into his greasy hands and scrubbing them. Only then did they notice that Althusser was gone.

There was no sign of him on the road, which left only the forest. There was the strip of bush between the highway and the lake, or the other one, the green wall of woods that stretched inland for who knew how many miles?

"The lake," said Jean Claude.

Greenberg saw no reason to debate this. They ranged along the roadside seeking some trail through the tangle of weedy undergrowth. Arms shielding his head, Jean Claude plunged in as if charging enemy fire. Greenberg followed, thorns snagging his sleeves and trousers, until they broke though to a boggy shore stamped with hoof prints and scattered with pebbly deer droppings. Peering around in the green-blue light they saw a few boats sitting landscape-still on the lake. Greenberg raised his hands to shout but Jean Claude touched his arm meaning no. He stood still and listened like a sculpture titled *Listener*. Through the treetops slid a light wind, near the ground was a stir of insects, to the left the lake breathed against the damp dark bank. With his chin, Jean Claude indicated the way. Greenberg followed, wishing he'd taken a bigger swig of that Scotch, wishing he'd wriggled out of Althusser's plea to join him on this fiasco. He should have insisted on flying to Emma Lake, told them he wanted a plane ticket—first class—or it was no go. Jean Claude moved with a tracker's stealth, placing his feet carefully, nimbly, in spite of the cast, brushing branches aside with the instinctive ease of a karate expert parrying kicks and punches.

"Does he swim?" whispered Greenberg.

"Louis?" The scorn in Jean Claude's voice was answer enough. He halted and crouched lower, peering. "There." He pointed to a clearing. They found Althusser sitting cross-legged, elbows on his knees, and chin on his clasped hands, studying something on the ground with the intensity of a monk meditating upon a flame. They approached slowly, Greenberg acutely aware of leaves and twigs crackling under the soles of his loafers that were now in serious need of a scrub and a polish.

"Regard," said Althusser, not looking up, but maintaining his focus on a dead rat under a living fur of wasps. The rat had already been reduced to a skull, spine, claws, and tail. Althusser reached out and slowly crushed one wasp under his forefinger. "The trick is to get them on the top. To sting they must curl their tail under. Like so. It is very satisfying to kill them. A dry crunch, like bones. They are fools, these creatures. Mindless. Willing to die for the colony."

"Like communists?" suggested Greenberg.

"Ha." Althusser laughed at the absurdity. "Yes, if only man's brain could be washed clean of its delusion of individuality. They are instructive, these creatures. And beautiful. Though cold, like science."

In the lakeside, half-light of the forest, Greenberg squatted on his haunches and gave in to studying the spectacle of seething wasps. He thought of a chemical process, the working of acids. Althusser was innocently, almost endearingly absorbed. Greenberg looked at Jean Claude expecting him to be charmed by his compatriot's child-like entrancement. And yet the expression he saw rocked him back: hatred. Not directed at Greenberg, nor at the blind frenzy of carnivorous insects, but at Althusser himself. Hatred. And in his hand—a blade? Greenberg squinted. Jean Claude slid something back up under his sweater, loudly cleared his throat, and with an enormous effort managed to twist his face into a smile.

"Yes, Louis," he said, indulgent, as if speaking to a child, "like science."

༺༅༻

An hour out of Duluth, they overtook a convoy of jeeps, trucks, and trailers bearing cannons and rocket launchers. Jean Claude swung out to pass and as he did, rows of soldiers in combat green seated in troop carriers eyed the blue Dodge and the three men inside.

"They are mobilizing," murmured Althusser.

"It is madness," said Jean Claude.

"It's theatre," said Greenberg.

"Of course it is theatre," said Althusser. "The theatre of the absurd." He lit his pipe. "Artaud. Beckett. These are our prophets now. And that albino. What is his name? War—"

"Warhol."

"A smart cookie that guy," said Louis in his best American. "There are no flies on him."

As they passed the lead jeep, the man in the passenger seat photographed them. Althusser gave them an enthusiastic thumbs up.

Thursday, 25 October, 1962

They passed the night in Duluth and were on the road early, angling their way northwest toward Saskatchewan. Greenberg had found a liquor store and now had two fifths of Jack Daniels wrapped in towels he'd stolen from the Howard Johnson stowed in his suitcase, and a third bottle, already half empty, with him in the back seat. He had devised and rejected various plans. Clouting Jean Claude across the back of the head with a whisky bottle was the most direct, but there would be blood and the car would be a mess. And it was hard to predict how Althusser would react. The nature of the relationship between the two Frenchmen bewildered him. What was clear was that there had been a knife in Jean Claude's hand and hatred on his face.

Had Jean Claude intended to stab Althusser right there in front of Greenberg? If so, then Jean Claude must have been prepared to kill Greenberg as well. Fear dripped like acid through his stomach and he rode out a wave of nausea. He put his hand to his brow: clammy. Then he spotted himself in Jean Claude's gaze in the rearview mirror. Was that a smile curling the corner of his mouth? Greenberg looked away. Now what?

Ditching Jean Claude a second time was unlikely. Why was Jean Claude not wearing a pistol in one of those under-the-arm holsters rather than packing a knife? Was he not a member of the French Secret Service? Was he not a bodyguard? Assassins and punks and thugs used knives; is that what Jean

Claude was, an assassin, a hired killer? But hired to kill who? Greenberg began to fear that he was he in over his head. How had life become so complicated?

As a kid, he'd had a jack knife, yet it was a sword that he had truly wanted, for they were heroic and honourable while a knife was sneaky. Iago had a stiletto and Othello had a sword. The three musketeers had swords. When he began looking seriously at paintings he often found himself paying particular attention to cutlasses and rapiers, scimitars and épées, appalled and impressed at the casualness of such raw violence so close to hand.

Althusser was at the radio again. There was live reporting from the destroyer *USS Joseph P Kennedy Jr.* as a search crew boarded the Lebanese freighter *Marcula* under charter by the Soviet Union.

"The masses will like this very much," said Althusser. "It will fuel the fires of patriotism. How brightly they will burn. They will see glory in sacrifice. When the missiles begin to fall, they will die singing while the politicians hide in their holes."

Greenberg studied the back of Althusser's shaved head, repulsed and fascinated by the corrugations in the lower skull. "I thought you believed in the masses."

"I have told you, I believe in science."

"The science of what?"

"Of everything."

"That means nothing. You're a walking contradiction."

"My friend, contradiction went out with Hegel. It is the human condition."

"Science is always in the service of the state and the state is always at war," said Greenberg.

"But you are a fool, Greenbairg. If not states then tribes, if not tribes then clans, if not clans then families, if not me—you."

Greenberg gave up. He looked at Jean Claude who seemed more glum than usual.

"You want me to take a turn at the wheel?" asked Greenberg.

"Fuck off."

Yes, he was definitely in over his head.

"I gotta piss," drawled Louis out the side of his mouth.

Jean Claude pulled into a rest stop. Althusser's time in a POW camp had weakened his bladder. So far he'd been brisk in his business, but this time he lingered after he'd finished and stood in a pensive attitude. Though the rest stop had a washroom, he preferred the great outdoors, and so stood facing a field as if it was his accuser. After a few minutes he raised his hands in a pleading gesture, then put them to his face as though fitting on a mask, his condemnation, his punishment. Greenberg, confused, embarrassed, looked away. There was only one other vehicle in the rest stop, a trucker, and as the man entered the washroom he regarded Althusser with suspicion. The wind intensified, gritty and cold. Greenberg, in the Dodge, saw it thrashing the tall grass and heard it beating against the car window, a wind coming out of the north warning of winter, the season of withdrawal and death, the white bear awaiting lost souls. Althusser, twenty yards from the car, kept his hands pressed to his face as if the wind and the prairie demanded a truthfulness he could not give. Were his shoulders shuddering, was he weeping? The trucker emerged from the washroom and again regarded Althusser. The expanse of land spreading wide in all directions made Greenberg think of settlers, Indians, the ice age, birds the size of biplanes that soared crying above primeval swamps. In Alberta and Saskatchewan they were finding dinosaur fossils all the time. Maybe the very land itself remembered all of this in some geologic fashion, and it was this that Althusser was sensing. Greenberg, watching, began to fear that Althusser would collapse and they'd have to deliver him shattered to the hospital, like a crate of bones for the doctors to reassemble.

Jean Claude was also watching, his face torqued into a grimace like some primitive mask. Yes, hatred. Greenberg quickly looked away, heart pounding.

When Althusser got back in the car they sat in silence, and in that moment Greenberg suspected that anything could happen, Jean Claude could pull that knife or Greenberg could suggest Mexico and Jean Claude would swing the car around and in a few days they'd be in Tijuana. A fork in the psychic road, a turning point, an opening in which they could each go their separate way. Yet the moment passed and Jean Claude started up and pulled onto the highway. Greenberg crossed his arms tightly over his chest, crossed his legs tightly at the knees and stared hard out the side window as the Dodge accelerated and the telephone poles ticked past and the wires swooped and rose. Hate. And a knife. He began shifting the chess pieces back a few moves. Althusser, Algerian-born, murderer, communist. Jean Claude, Algerian-born, his Vietnamese wife murdered by communists in Saigon. Althusser had explained all this and more to Greenberg. Jean Claude had apparently been so devastated by the death of his wife he'd had a breakdown, railing against Mao and Marxists, vowing revenge. Which begged the question: why put a commie in the care of a commie hater?

Seated in the right rear corner of the car, Greenberg studied the back of Jean Claude's head with its thick dark hair, and then Althusser's shaved and corrugated nape. The arrangement had been sudden, a last minute call from Paris, hurried and furtive, Althusser pleading with Greenberg to join him on this cross-country tour. That had been his word, tour. Or had it been escapade? Either way, the synchronicity had been undeniable, Greenberg's plans already set, Weyburn and Emma Lake in the same province, and Rosenberg a splinter in his soul needing to be pulled—who better than Louis to do it? Still, he'd been hesitant, not exactly comfortable with the idea of five days in a car with a man he'd known only briefly seven years ago, a man who'd strangled his wife and been declared insane and was now en route for LSD treatment in a Canadian madhouse. On the other hand he couldn't deny being flattered that Althusser had called him. Certainly it was better him than Rosenberg. God, how Rosenberg would have gloated! Greenberg had told a few people—fifty or sixty—just to be sure Rosenberg heard. Ha. With Camus gone who but Sartre was more renowned than Althusser? But there'd been no mention of Jean Claude.

Greenberg stared harder out the window. They were passing beyond the Great Lakes Basin and rising gradually onto the Great Plains, the colours draining with the season and the geology. He looked at the neck of his whisky bottle under the seat, thought of those five Tuinals nestled in his coat pocket and longed for the sweet oblivion of dreamless sleep. All he wanted was to go to studios and galleries and look at art, go home and write about art, attend cocktail parties and drink and talk about art, and then maybe afterwards have a little sex if the mood took him, and of course kill Rosenberg. Was this too much to ask?

The sun sank bloated as a rotting pumpkin. They drove on, angling their way into the deepening dusk and pulled in at a town called Haaden Creek, a few shops, a stuffed bear on wheels wearing a Chicago Cubs baseball cap in front of a tavern called Smokey's. Some fifty yards further up the highway was a stream spanned by an iron bridge.

Greenberg and Jean Claude stood on either side of the Dodge and smoked while Althusser hurried off along a creekside path to relieve himself again. Jean Claude smoked Gitanes; Greenberg lit one of his Camels. The heat in his chest was welcome. The autumn chill hardened the air and he snugged his coat—charcoal with a steep lapel and fine gold stripe—not heavy enough for the prairie weather but the cut made him feel suave and hid his paunch.

As he smoked, he mulled. What if he let Jean Claude go ahead and do what he wanted—and then in order to earn Greenberg's silence knocked off Rosenberg for him? After all, did it matter which Frenchman did the deed? But how could he be sure he'd seen what he thought he'd seen, how could he be certain Jean Claude was an assassin whose target was Althusser? There'd definitely been a knife, yes, of that he was sure, and that expression had been hate—or was it merely the pain in his foot, or the memory of his wife's death?

Airily, offhand, Greenberg asked, "How long have you and Althusser known each other?"

"Since before we were born."

Greenberg expected some sort of sour Gallic grimace, but there was nothing. He waited a few moments. "How did you end up here on this…assignment?"

Jean Claude gazed off, smoke seeping from his nostrils as if in spite of his seeming calm his brain was smouldering.

Greenberg plunged ahead. "I think we both know that this is a one-way trip for Louis."

Jean Claude shrugged with elaborate nonchalance.

Was he being too direct? "There was news coverage here. 'Infamous French Marxist strangles wife.' A lot of talk at cocktail parties. Many people thought he deserved the electric chair, or the guillotine."

Jean Claude blew a smoke ring and was silent. Greenberg was about to change tack when Jean Claude said, "The French respect fame more than money. He has many admirers, our Louis. But there are many who—" He blew another smoke ring then shattered it with a backhand.

"A commie," said Greenberg.

Jean Claude stood in profile. He raised his chin as if to elevate his nose above a creeping stench.

"I suppose there are some people who'd like to see him simply disappear. Maybe a lot of people."

Now Jean Claude's right eyebrow arced and he turned his head to regard Greenberg full on.

Greenberg waited.

Jean Claude waited.

"Will it look like an accident?"

Not a flicker.

Time was ticking. Althusser would be finished his business. "Suicide?"

Jean Claude's nostrils opened while his thin lips shaped themselves into a wry smile.

Greenberg said, "You do what you have to do." He shrugged implying that he understood these things, that there was no judgment.

"Who are you talking about?"

Greenberg tried not to sound flustered. "Anyone. Everyone. Me. You."

"I do what I do."

"Of course. Fine. You're a pro."

"Thank you."

"Except, I mean, there's me."

Now Jean Claude laughed silently as if the truth was coming out at long last. "And who are you?"

Was this *Godot*? "I'm me."

Jean Claude shrugged at such an insignificant detail.

"I won't say anything. But, you know, tit for tat."

"Tit?"

"For tat. A price for everything."

Jean Claude inhaled the last of his cigarette, dropped it, stepped on it and exhaled a weary sigh of smoke. "Black-mail."

Greenberg winced at such bluntness. "Cooperation. One deed for another." But he was exultant, too. Jean Claude had all but admitted the truth.

"Who is the target?"

Greenberg sketched Rosenberg's salient points.

"Eliminate the competition."

"Exactly."

"But what makes you think I am planning to kill our poor Louis?"

Greenberg fought not to gulp. Had Jean Claude suckered him, let him expose himself? What an amateur!

"If I was planning to do this thing—*if*—why do I not simply kill you, too. Eh?" He smiled. It was a surprisingly open, if not exactly innocent or ingenuous, smile, one in which Greenberg glimpsed a much younger Jean Claude, one who had once envisioned a future with the woman he loved, the woman who had been murdered.

"Kill me?" Greenberg feigned surprise.

"But it is obvious. *Pop*. No more witness. This Rosenberg has done nothing to me while you, you break my toe."

"I'll pay you," said Greenberg.

"Now we are talking."

"Do you like art?"

"I am French."

"I have an art collection."

"You are offering me a picture."

Was that scorn? Greenberg was indignant. French or not, Jean Claude was a boor. "I can sell some paintings and pay you American dollars."

Jean Claude studied the sky. "Murder is not easy."

"Consider it execution."

"It is no different." What weariness there was in his tone; he had been here before.

From the far side of the car Greenberg studied Jean Claude and wondered what Rodin would do with the bone structure, how his eye would glide and his hand would contour. Jean Claude lit up another Gitane and made it crackle. Greenberg imagined him in Southeast Asia, clad in a sarong and flip-flops, geckos pulsing on the bamboo posts and mahogany walls of a house in a jungle in the black pepper night, his slim wife beckoning...

"So you'll do it."

"Ten thousand."

Greenberg felt raped. He saw scars on the walls where paintings he would be forced to sacrifice had hung, but already his mind was calculating, drawing up a list of works he was willing to part with, estimating prices and buyers, tabulating even as he reassured himself that the Newmans and Pollocks would stay.

"And the car," said Jean Claude. "I take the Dodge."

"It's a rental."

Jean Claude caressed the hood with the backs of his knuckles. "Tell them it was stolen."

"There's a damage deposit," said Greenberg, trying not to whine. "And a penalty charge."

Jean Claude was watching Althusser coming toward them along the creekside path. "That is your problem." He scratched his belly in a leisurely fashion. "All this talk has made me thirsty. Come, we go to the tavern."

❧

The dominant motif was wood, the tables and chairs, the posts that held cross beams of raw logs, and the bar itself which was a varnished forty-foot plank, the tongue and groove floor strewn with sawdust, while the air was a broth of beer and sweat and cigarettes. It was Friday afternoon and Smokey's was crowded with men thirsty after a week's farm labour. The arrival of three strangers was noted. Some men nodded and even touched the brims of their caps while others made a point of turning away. The couture consisted of denim jackets, denim pants, denim overalls, Stetsons, and ball caps with CAT and John Deere stitched on the front.

Greenberg felt alien, a Jew gazing at the massing storm cloud of the goyim.

Jean Claude steered them to a table by the wall.

Nearby, a jukebox blinked mutely, like a sad and forgotten robot, for all eyes were on the TV above the bar where a newsman explained how four Soviet submarines had changed course to head back across the Atlantic. It was too soon for celebration, however, for there was another sub, identified only as B-36, which US Navy spotter planes claimed was not turning back, "but proceeding," said the announcer, "grimly, inexorably, like the course of a disease, an infection, malignant and remorseless, in a southerly direction toward Haiti at a speed of seven knots." Footage showed the sub's conning tower on which were stencilled in large white numbers: 911. Other footage showed Skyhawks making passes like enraged blue jays over the B-36 as it submerged into a foaming sea.

"As of yet neither Moscow nor the Soviet embassy in Washington have offered explanation or comment."

No such reticence hindered the patrons of Smokey's.

"That baby's packing."

"Long as Soldier Field, that mother."

"Can't even build a bicycle and now they're playing with nukes."

"Put a man in space. Beat us on that one," said a cautionary voice.

"Let me tell you about bicycles. I got a cousin from Chicago who was in Warsaw in '45. Said those Reds were all crowding around a bicycle. A bicycle! Looking at it like a bunch of monkeys. First time they'd ever seen one. Medieval people. Ignorant as all get-out."

"Willfully blinkered."

"Steal secrets and kidnap scientists is how they work."

"That's how they beat us into space."

"And now those Cuban spics."

"Jack'll sort their refried beans. You watch."

"I tell you this—Ike wouldn't stand for it."

A waiter arrived, beard reaching mid-bib of his overalls, the very sight of his scrub brush crewcut causing Greenberg's skin to itch. "Can I bring you fellas a beverage?"

"A jug of beer and three double whiskys," said Greenberg.

"Bar Scotch suit you?"

"Bar Scotch'll suit us fine."

Noting Althusser's maple leaf toque, he said, "Canuckers are yuh?"

Greenberg nodded and smiled as if to say you caught us.

"Welcome to Haaden Creek."

"Thank you. Where's the washroom?"

The waiter pointed.

Greenberg weaved his way between the tables and into the john whose walls were hung with stained photos of logging equipment, skidders and winches and men at either end of long saws. He ran hot water in the coved porcelain basin and washed his face then studied the towel for an unsullied corner. Finding none, he unspooled paper from the toilet roll and dried off. So, he and Jean Claude had an accord, they were accomplices. He felt sick and terrified and exhilarated as well as guilty at betraying Louis. But were they friends, really? A few days in Paris years ago? And wasn't the guy a murderer, a wife killer? Had he not endorsed Stalin? Was he not a commie? Whatever happened to justice? Clearly the French brass wanted to see the back of him. Someone had had enough of Althusser's Marxist pronouncements and was willing to pay Jean Claude to escort him out of the country and shut him up. Who was Greenberg to stand in the way?

When this was over Bud Gregory would write a bestseller and dedicate it to, well, maybe he'd damn well dedicate it to himself! He returned to the table where the drinks were waiting. He filled his glass with draft, gulped the whisky, chased it with beer and felt like an exhausted swimmer whose toes had at long last touched shore.

The commentator was summing up the state of the crisis. "...Monday last the president stated that 'establishing a quarantine around Cuba was only the first step in American measures to force Khrushchev to withdraw his missiles. If he fails to do so then further actions may be justified.' Those were his words. Well, it seems to this reporter that such measures, whatever form they may take, are more than justified, for the Soviets—trafficking in typical Red double-speak—continue to deny even the presence of missiles."

A rolling thunder of murmurs vibrated through Smokey's. Greenberg had voted for JFK but worried that he listened too closely to his brother Bobby who was squirrelly and erratic and all too high strung to be advising on serious policy decisions. Jack was more stable, but he had health problems, and rumour was that his sex addiction was draining his vital energies. He was a man, flesh and blood, but he had duties and obligations. Still, he looked better than Nixon, he had class and great teeth, and the aura of honour and even nobility what with his service record, but when it came to dealing with the Russians maybe you needed someone willing to kick and gouge and play dirty, someone able to ignore the rules just the way the enemy was doing.

The post-war relief had always been tainted by the red cloud smouldering on the eastern horizon. Greenberg imagined the Soviets as a headless corpse that, animated by some primordial virus, some blind Asiatic fanaticism melding with medieval Slavic imbecility, continued to grope zombie-like over the land.

Now White House press secretary Pierre Salinger was affirming the continuing build-up of missile sites on Cuba. Salinger was fat, had a long nose and oily dark hair. Greenberg had met him once; he smelled of earwax.

"We are in the hands of the Three Stooges," said Althusser. A few heads turned.

"I think Khrushchev is Moe," he continued in a rising voice. "Always in a bad temper. And of course Castro must be Larry. All that hair. Which leaves JFK as Curly." Suddenly ingenuous, Althusser turned to Greenberg and asked if he had ever heard his definition of madness?

Greenberg managed to croak, "No."

"No?" Althusser seemed genuinely bewildered.

Through clenched teeth Jean Claude hissed, "Shut up."

Althusser ignored this. Perhaps it was the medication, but for a Frenchman he seemed strangely susceptible to alcohol, drunk already, and not about to leave Smokey's before delivering his lecture. Settling himself in his chair his English took on a new and orotund fluency that suggested a well-rehearsed speech. "Or rather let us speak of sanity," he began. "Sanity is like a man balancing on top of a ball. Do not ask if this sanity resides in the man or in the ball. It is in the relationship between the two. The sane man maintains balance on top of the ball by virtue of his self-control. I speak of course of mental control. He does not venture too far in any direction. He is not imaginative. He stays still. Like the cow in the field he moves little, he stays where the grass is green because sanity is for the herd, for the mediocre, for the cautious, for the dull of mind and small of soul. For once he takes a step in any direction, our cow, our bovine, our bourgeois, he falls. Once fallen, climbing back up onto the ball is almost impossible. Especially inasmuch as he brings with him the memory of having fallen, of having left the herd. He will be forever haunted by the abyss into which he had tumbled and wandered, lost and raving. Like the man in Munch's *Scream*, he is possessed, and this memory, this devil in his soul destabilizes him forever more. On this I can speak with authority." Finished, Althusser smiled tragically and drank his beer. Then he raised his right hand as though brandishing a torch in the darkest night and cried, "Viva la revolución!" And he slammed the hand down causing the beer jug to jump from the table and burst on the floor.

In an instant Jean Claude was pulling Althusser to his feet and apologizing to the patrons who had turned en masse from the TV. He tried pushing Althusser toward the door but the madman shimmied from his grip and, free, straightened his coat then strolled around the table, took Jean Claude's seat and called for more whisky and more beer. "*Allez! Vite!*"

The bearded waiter arrived with a box of sawdust, a broom, and a dustpan. Althusser raised his feet to oblige and, offering regrets for his unforgivable clumsiness, admired the man's technique as he cleaned the mess.

"I am a fool. I do not hold my liquor well. It is very un-French. *Je suis désolé.*"

"You French are you?"

"Yes." He looked left then right, then leaned conspiratorially toward the waiter who held a dustpan loaded with broken glass. "And a murderer."

Every face in the tavern watched this scene even as the TV showed footage of American jets and Soviet submarines. The waiter closed one eye and directed his good ear toward this stranger. "Who did you murder?"

"My wife."

A snort of laughter came from a nearby table. "Should be a reward for that." Failing to win any camaraderie the wag self-consciously cleared his throat and grew stern.

Still holding the pan of shattered glass, the waiter asked, "Why would you go and do something like that?"

At this Althusser raised his frail shoulders and, defeated, let them drop. His gaze searched the table as though the answer might be found amid the dark knots that resembled the unblinking eyes of his accusers. "This is a beautiful piece of wood," he said, and stroked it almost tearfully.

"Pine."

"You are married?"

"Yessir."

"Children?"

"Boy and a girl. He's in the service and she's teaching school."

Althusser closed his eyes and tilted his head in rapture. "But this is wonderful, my friend. Family is everything. Let me kiss you!"

Ignoring this, the waiter drew away and lowered his voice, "You know you ought not to talk about revolution."

"He's distraught," explained Greenberg taking the waiter aside. "Not a well man. The war. A prisoner. Shell shock. Never recovered."

With his dustpan of broken glass sparking blue and yellow and green in the tavern's smokey light, the waiter resembled some gold panner of yore. "I seen some things I'd rather not of myself." Then he added in a lower tone, "This is a small town. Folks have their ways. No offense, but you might well consider it prudent to pay up and move on."

"But we are possessed of a powerful thirst," lamented Althusser. "I am buying everyone a drink! We must bear witness to history. Look." He pointed at Walter Cronkite's face filling the TV screen.

"At this very moment Premier Khrushchev is in communication with President Kennedy. The exact nature of the communication has yet to be revealed though sources close to the White House suggest that the Soviet leader is warning of dire consequences should the US launch an attack on Cuba. Indeed the Soviet-Cuban alliance expect an invasion to begin this very night, first with an air assault and then with ground troops numbering in the tens of thousands. The fate of the Western world would seem to be in the balance as these three men—" (head shots of Kennedy, Khrushchev, and Castro side-by-side on the screen) "—attempt to loosen this Gordian knot, to thaw this iceberg, to negotiate a pathway through a nuclear minefield whose repercussions will be felt around the globe and for decades, perhaps centuries, to come."

"Monkeys!" shouted Althusser.

Jean Claude gripped Althusser's forearm.

"Goats and monkeys! Off with their heads!"

Faces stared, some blank, some confused, many angry. From out of their silence came a strange voice, quiet but clear, almost mechanical, "Call Swen," it said.

No one seemed to hear.

The waiter said, "You fellas do grasp the real and distinct possibility that the world as we know it may well and truly go up in flames this very night?"

Althusser pressed his fists to his chest. "It is the Rapture! We will all go up together. Let me kiss you. Let me kiss you all!"

"Swen should be here," said the strange voice. It had the timbre of a recording, realistic but not quite right.

The only one to move was the bartender. Visible from the waist up, he slid like a shooting gallery decoy to the telephone where he dialled and waited and then spoke, all the while staring at Greenberg, Althusser, and Jean Claude. He nodded once and replaced the receiver in its cradle and announced in a dread voice, "Swen's coming."

There was a stir, like a sudden wind from no one direction.

"Who is this Swen?" called Althusser loud enough for the entire tavern to hear.

"We should go," said Greenberg.

The strange voice said, "The time for going is gone. Now it's time for Swen...Donald."

Donald the bartender barred the door with a plank.

The man with the voice emerged from the tables. He stood about five foot six, a bald and androgynous creature lacking both eyebrows and eyelashes, his ears small and his eyes large, wearing a shiny green jumpsuit that zipped to the neck.

Greenberg's scrotum shrank and a metallic taste coppered his throat.

The man said, "Sit."

Greenberg sat.

The man's words seemed to arise from some place other than his body, as if he was a conduit to a distant source. His eyes had a fish-like flatness and rarely blinked. His left arm rose as though drawn by a string and the limp-wristed hand pointed—forefinger long and sharp nailed—toward the door. "Swen will be here soon."

The tavern fell still but for the drift of cigarette smoke. Greenberg felt strange, lightheaded but alert, as he often did after the first couple of drinks, but this was different, almost psychotropic. He looked at Althusser and Jean Claude and they too seemed disturbed. His mind slowed like a river reaching a slough whose green and fecund waters bred images that crawled forth to stand upright and forlorn: child victims of TB and influenza, wan-eyed creatures gazing from the dusklands between Heaven and Hell, neither tormented nor praised, neither warm nor cold, creatures adrift in shadow as grey as the smoke in the tavern where Greenberg sensed that he was being penetrated by a gaze that was piercing and pervasive, enveloping and incandescent, and he had a vision of a photographer's darkroom lit with infrared light as a picture emerged from the sloshing brew of a developer's tray, the image gradual, advancing and then retreating in tints and lines, to finally coalesce as Greenberg's own face gazing as enigmatic and ageless as an Olmec head, except that even as he watched his eyes opened and focused on him, his own eyes viewing him through his own eyes, a Möbius strip mirror in which he looked simultaneously outward and inward.

Someone coughed. Greenberg blinked. Time resumed and from outside came the slow crunch of car tires on gravel, then a door opening and closing followed by footsteps. Donald-the-bartender slid the plank from its brackets and a man flowed into the room with a momentum begun the day he was born. The man did not need to pause or look around or ask questions to know what was what. He walked straight to their table.

"Bob? These them?"

Bob, the baldy in the jumpsuit, blinked once as if changing the station on a television. "As the sky is blue."

Swen took a moment to regard Bob, and frowned in bemusement before returning his attention to the task at hand, the three strangers. Swen was not a large man. The tavern light ran in his greying blond hair. His goatee was impeccable, his nose thin and straight, his eyes aluminum. He wore a short-waisted denim jacket of dark blue and he was fit, impressively shouldered, flat-stomached, narrow-hipped, wearing a belt whose buckle was a galloping mustang. His oxblood riding boots were gleaming. For all his formidable presence, however, he stood with his hands lightly clasped one atop the other in the manner of a matron welcoming guests to afternoon tea. "Am I to understand that we have a situation?"

"We were just leaving," said Greenberg.

Jean Claude took a step but Swen extended his arm gate-like to halt him. Greenberg was surprised to see Jean Claude so easily stopped.

Swen spoke softly. His velvety voice recalled Mel Torme. "You in a hurry?"

"We're on the road," said Greenberg.

"In which direction?" Swen lowered the barrier of his arm and tilted his head in polite interest.

Greenberg did not hesitate. "South."

"South?"

"South-west. The coast. Los Angeles."

"The angels." Swen nodded deeply as if this put a fresh spin on the case, a reaction that made Greenberg regret his choice of city. Swen seemed to reach a conclusion. "Gentlemen, as this is a police matter, it is appropriate to convene our investigation to more secure quarters." He directed them toward the bar.

Greenberg, Jean Claude, and Althusser looked at each other in confusion: was Swen buying them a round, is this the way it was done in such outland regions?

They joined the bartender in his narrow workplace behind the counter and watched the man heave open a hatch in the floor unleashing an odour of bleach and concrete. Althusser tried backing away yet found himself corralled by the waiter who was now holding a fire axe. Althusser had gone a shade of green more suited to an amphibian than a human. Greenberg suspected he was recalling the punishment hole in the camp, while Jean Claude saw a cell used to break the defiance of Viet Minh, a cell where he had done the breaking. Greenberg did not envision interrogation and torture but a chute where they would be set adrift like astronauts exiled to deepest space.

Swen seemed to appreciate the grim inspirational nature of this hole and he allowed time for their minds to spin to fullest effect. Finally he nodded and the bartender pushed a light switch and a glow filled the hole like some vapourish mildew. Swen began descending the iron ladder hung from the side. It put Greenberg in mind of a conning tower. When Swen's head was floor-level, he paused and Greenberg thought briefly of kicking him in the face, but Swen said, "Nice shoes." Greenberg looked at his tan Hush Puppies and experienced the panic that occasionally came when he smoked tea after he'd been drinking. It was okay to smoke tea and then drink, but the other way around inevitably made him ill with anxiety, and that was what he felt now.

"Thank you."

"They provide good arch support, do they?"

For a moment Greenberg did not grasp what Swen was saying. "Yes. Very good."

"I have no end of troubles with my feet. I'll have to try a pair. Gentlemen. Follow me."

Greenberg looked around thinking he might vault the bar and bolt for the door, but the entire tavern was watching. He began descending the cold iron rungs. When he was nose-level with the tavern floor, he noted Bob's shoes, which looked like gloves, his feet slender and shapely, the leather like skin over them. Greenberg wondered if Bob was in fact a woman, or something else altogether. His gaze travelled up the length of

Bob's zippered jumpsuit to linger upon his thin-chinned, small-eared, fish-eyed face. Then the floor eclipsed Bob, and Greenberg continued his descent.

It could easily have been mistaken for a rumpus room but for the shelves stocked with canned goods and jugs of bleach. Something about the tinned goods was troubling. The walls were panelled in pale pine as was the floor and the surprisingly high ceiling. The preponderance of eye-like knots gave Greenberg the sense of being watched, that the very room itself was alive, a thousand-eyed creature contemplating ensnared prey before consuming it.

Bob was the last to descend the ladder and he did so with the slow and exaggerated litheness of Marcel Marceau pretending to descend a ladder.

Swen was gracious. "Gentlemen. Be seated."

They sat on a low Danish modern sofa covered in burgundy burlap, the legs and arms walnut-stained wood. Against the wall opposite stood bookshelves flanked by lamps with milk-glass globes, the shelves stocked with *Popular Mechanics* and a leather-bound edition of the *Harvard Classics*. To both the left and the right, the room receded into darkness. As with the tavern above, raw logs two feet thick supported the ceiling. From somewhere came a muted vibration that Greenberg assumed must be a generator.

Swen corralled a chair and positioned it so as to face his guests. He sat comfortably, legs crossed at the knees, hands folded in his lap, a smile shaping his mouth though leaving his cool blue eyes oddly inert. Greenberg fought to stay calm and think clearly. Swen appeared a patriot, a man of core values and gravitas, rooted in faith in the soil, in the blood and destiny of the New Continent foretold in the Testaments, the base camp in the American ascent to the Summit of Being. Greenberg was not utterly immune to patriotism, he was not above saluting the flag or feeling a swell in his chest when he heard the anthem, but at the moment he would give anything to be seated in a sunny piazza in Rome sipping a Cinzano and soda, an afternoon of gallery hopping ahead of him. Or failing that sitting at home with a Scotch and a book.

"So you say you're headed to the city of angels."

"Yes."

"South by south-west."

Greenberg nodded.

"And yet," said Swen, reaching into the inner pocket of his tailored denim jacket and coming out with a sheet of paper. "It says here that you, Clement Greenberg—is that you?"

Greenberg nodded.

"Rented that fine Dodge in New York City at...six a.m. Monday the twenty-second of October in this year of our Lord. Which puts you as heading not south by southwest but north by northwest." Swen looked first at Greenberg, then Althusser, and then Jean Claude, and then at Greenberg again while affably awaiting an explanation.

"We are lost," croaked Althusser.

"Lost?"

"We take the wrong turn."

"Well that does indeed happen," allowed Swen. "Do I detect an accent *française*?"

"It is no crime."

"Well not yet," grinned Swen. "But you were spouting some troubling remarks earlier no matter what the accent."

"He's drunk," said Greenberg.

"According to Donald, you shared a jug of beer. Three men, one jug, hardly over the top, I'd say."

"And whisky," said Jean Claude. "We drink whisky."

"Now why would you be heading to Los Angeles via this roundabout route?"

"Taking our time," said Greenberg. "Sightseeing."

"What sort of sights? Missile silos?"

"Pardon me?"

"Uranium deposits?"

"We don't—"

"You know you two could be brothers." Swen's finger ticked side to side indicating Jean Claude and Althusser. "Though this fella, he doesn't look too top of the trees."

"I am sick," croaked Althusser.

Swen was not unsympathetic. "I was down with a nasty cold until last week," he said. "Threatened to go into my chest." He put his palm to his heart then brightened. "So. How do you all happen to be travelling together? Pals? Colleagues? ...Comrades?"

"Paris," said Greenberg. "We met in Paris."

"Well that is indeed a beautiful city. I am partial to the cathedrals. And Versailles. Who could not be impressed by Versailles? My wife is taking a Berlitz course in French. She's all *parlez-vous* this and *parlez-vous* that. Has every intention of our taking a vacation there. Itinerary already planned. Are you familiar with the Communist Control Act? Specifically statute sixty-eight? No? Ike signed it into law in '54. Goes like this: it is a criminal offence to be a member in, or act in support of, the Communist Party. So I am wondering about your remarks earlier this evening." From another pocket Swen drew a note pad and flipped it open. "Let's see, 'Vive la revolution!' And here, 'I am a murderer.' And this other one, oh yes, 'Let me kiss you all.'" Swen looked at them. "I'm wondering if you can explain these remarks. Because what I see, and I think what any reasonable mind would conclude, is that we've got revolution, murder, and, even allowing for your *ways française*, homosexual overtures, that is to say three fairly serious crimes, all rolled up in one ball named...what is your name, sir?"

"Louis Althusser."

"... Named Looee Altoozare. And associates who are aiders and abettors to said crimes. What do you think?"

"I think I need to pee," said Althusser.

Swen sat back and pointed. "Of course. First door on your right."

Althusser stood, wobbled—reached for Jean Claude's shoulder to steady himself—then moved like a man unused to legs in the direction Swen had indicated. When he reached the door and gripped the knob he froze.

"You have to push the door after you turn the knob, Looee."

Althusser managed a nod of acknowledgement, then stepped in and shut the door.

Greenberg saw what it was about the shelves of tinned food that had disturbed him: they were tins of Campbell's Soup. That little albino prick Warhol. This was all planned by fate, by the gods, those eternally adolescent Greek demons who were greedy and jealous and above all else bored. Or it was all Rosenberg's doing. A ludicrously paranoid theory but Greenberg couldn't help himself. The bastard knew Greenberg's schedule, knew he was en route and would do anything to disrupt him, a few phone calls is all it would take, a few not so subtle remarks and one, two, three, he'd be derailed. The man would do anything to prevent him from reaching Emma Lake. This was typical, this was the way Rosenberg operated. It fairly stank of the bastard; the evil operator was desperate to have the Emma Lake gig all to himself.

Swen was carrying on about Bolshevism, which led to Saskatchewan. "A communist province in the middle of your otherwise decent nation. You call it socialism, as if it were the best of both worlds, the ideal compromise, one from column A and one from column B, but so do the Soviets term their own system a socialist republic, and so with the Vietnamese and the

Chinese. Yet I fear that the domino is poised to fall, and once one goes so too will the other provinces, Alberta to the west and Manitoba to the east, and after Alberta then British Columbia, and after Manitoba then Ontario. It began with socialized medicine. That's always the first move because it seems so benign." Swen shrugged massively. "Who would deny medical care to people? What doctor would turn away a suffering child? Let me tell you something. I have met premier Tommy Douglas. I have spoken at length with him. And you know what? I like him. Like the hell out of him. I do not agree with him, but I see a man of gracious manner and well-spoken conviction. I could very well call him friend if he were not so willfully out to rob me and my family and my countrymen of our rights as free and active agents in our very own lives." Swen opened his arms in a gesture that appealed for under-standing, a gesture that asked if his position lacked merit.

If it came to a choice between this Tommy Douglas and Swen, well, given the present circumstances, Greenberg was Swen's man. He felt some small hopefulness at the eloquence with which Swen spoke, even if eloquence was rarely syn-onymous with kindness. Greenberg's socialist convictions had never been passionate, as often as not a means to advance his career and/or promote his penis, even if there was a lingering loyalty to the concept of shared resources. Then there was his vision of himself in a socialist system as Art Czar. No toiling in the fields for him. He'd never been to Russia, yet admired the look of Cyrillic, had gazed awestruck at pictures of the Volga in flood, and could see himself in an *astrakhan* hat and fur collar, sipping chilled vodka and nibbling caviar harvested from Caspian sturgeon, spending his evenings in Odessa cafés, or in a *dacha* in Sochi when not touring the tea estates of Georgia. In fact, he had notes for an essay tracing the roots of Abstract Expressionism back through Braque and Cézanne all the way to Pietr of Kiev, a fourteenth-century monk who experienced no fewer than three hallucinogenic episodes from eating bread baked with rye flour tainted by the ergot fungus and then travelled as far as Budapest and Prague preaching and painting en route.

Swen was frowning toward the door through which Althusser had disappeared.

Greenberg said, "His plumbing's not what it should be. I'll see what's up." As he approached the door he tried to see just how big the place was, but it was too dark. Did he sense something down there, a presence? Were there men in cells or shackled to walls? He glanced back at Swen and Jean Claude who were watching. He tapped the lavatory door. Adopting an affable tone, he asked, "How's it going in there, Louis?" Nothing. He tried the knob. It turned, but when he pushed he felt resistance. Shoving it part way open, he found Althusser braced against it, peering out at him.

"Greenbairg," he whispered. "Have you been to Dahomey?"

"Dahomey? No."

Althusser strained to glimpse Swen and Jean Claude. "It is like Haiti. There are zombies."

"I don't think there are zombies here."

"What about that one in the suit?"

Greenberg glanced at Bob standing at attention by the ladder.

"How are we doing, gentlemen?" called Swen.

Greenberg took Althusser's arm and drew him out and guided him back to the others.

"To proceed," said Swen.

Greenberg saw no way out but via the truth. He felt a rush of freedom, of cleanliness, of innocence, and wondered if this was what Catholics experienced when they went to confession? With a rush of hope, he began explaining that they were escorting Althusser to the hospital in Weyburn. "He's had a breakdown. Not his first. He's fragile."

"My mind is glass," admitted Althusser.

"He was a POW," added Greenberg.

"Claude glass," said Althusser. "Clear but dark. That is me, clear but dark."

"He killed his wife," said Greenberg, "a fit of madness." Fearing he'd blundered and said too much, he added quickly, "He went to trial. He's an important man in France. Very important. A philosopher. They want to see him cured. And in Weyburn, there's a hospital pioneering new treatments."

"Communist, murderer, homo, *and* madman," said Swen, smiling at the aces turning up in his hand. "In football—you are familiar with the game—in football, four downs and you lose the ball."

"Or we could just leave the field," said Greenberg. "So to speak. Never to be heard from again."

Swen mused. "Under calmer circumstances I might well go for that. No harm, no foul. But as I'm sure you're aware these are not calm circumstances—we're on the verge of war. How would it look if I let *agents provocateurs* go their merry way?"

Jean Claude, quiet until now, slapped his knee in frustration. "But we are not agents! We are nothing."

"*Mon ami*, I'm afraid nothing is nothing, not even nothing. Would that it were," Swen said ruefully. "I do believe your Monsieur Sartre made that point ad nauseum. No, I believe it only prudent to let you cool your heels here for the night. Keep you on the sidelines and out of trouble. In the morning I'll make a few phone calls, find out what's what and who's who. Best for everyone. Isn't that right, Bob?"

As still and silent as a caryatid, Bob now blinked and breathed. His mouth opened then shut. It opened again and he said, "Damn straight."

Swen did a wry double take reevaluating Bob. "Right."
Swen pressed his hands down on his knees and prepared to
rise but froze at the wail of a siren—many sirens—and then a
booming as of bombs. He remained in a half crouch as the
shelter began to rumble and books and tins vibrated on the
shelves. In an instant Bob was up the ladder with that strange
elastic grace, Swen right behind him. Althusser cringed with
his arms over his head in a pose that once again put Greenberg
in mind of Marcel Marceau, this tableau titled: *Apocalypse
From Above*. Jean Claude leapt to the foot of the ladder and
peered up while holding his hand palm outward meaning
wait. Greenberg's heartbeat staggered. Althusser moaned.
Jean Claude slowly ascended, rung by cautious rung. Silence.
Then a hissed signal. Greenberg hoisted Althusser to his feet
and dragged him to the ladder. They peered up. Jean Claude's
head was silhouetted in the square of light.

"Vite!"

They climbed and in seconds were beside Jean Claude peering Kilroy fashion over the bar. Everyone was at the door.
Men crouched, men upright, men down on their hands and
knees as if too weak to stand, one swooning, one with his
right arm raised as though in an appeal to the Lord...it was
a tableau out of Géricault or Bosch.

The booming vibrations continued.

Jean Claude put his finger to his lips then gestured and they
ran in a crouch toward the washrooms, Greenberg bumping
a table en route, but the soundwas swallowed in the massive
rumbling. In the bathroom they found the back door locked.

"Kick it!" said Althusser.

Jean Claude pointed to the cast on his foot.

Greenberg shoved open a window above the toilet and then
he and Jean Claude hoisted Althusser upside down so that his
feet went out the window first. Althusser slid through and

dropped with a small cry. There came a commotion from the tavern. Chairs and tables toppled. From either side of the toilet bowl Greenberg and Jean Claude looked at each other. Greenberg saw Jean Claude's mettle; Jean Claude saw Greenberg's fear. Jean Claude knew fear. When they'd come for Ha ng, his first reaction had been to beg, to offer money, to offer himself, his fingers, an eye, military secrets, anything. There had been no opportunity to reach for his gun. Two men had caught him by the elbows and wrenched them back dislocating his shoulders. He'd dropped to his knees cracking the patella of his right. The pain had been blinding but he'd looked up in time to see them drag Ha ng out. She managed a look over her shoulder, long black hair swirling like a dancer's skirt. Those dark eyes. Their lament. Ha ng. Vietnamese for angel in the full moon. Jean Claude reached across the toilet and gripped Greenberg's shoulder to strengthen him, then nodded to the window. "Go!"

Squeezing through the window frame, his buttocks and then belly reshaping, his ribs pressed and shoulders swivelling in their sockets, Greenberg felt like meat being extruded through a press. He dropped to the ground by Althusser who was lying on his back clutching his foot and moaning. "I am broken."

Jean Claude landed nimbly in spite of the cast, and set about palping Althusser's ankle. He drew him upright. "A sprain." When Althusser began to protest, Jean Claude closed a hand over his mouth, silencing him. Greenberg peered around the corner and saw a convoy of vehicles passing the tavern. Tanks and jeeps and troop carriers crossed the iron bridge over the creek in a cannonade of wheels that rumbled like mortar fire and grenades. Supporting Althusser, Jean Claude led the way into the bush. The sky had cleared and a half moon threw the complex shadows of slender trees over the leafy ground.

"What about the car?" said Greenberg.

"The car is lost," said Jean Claude.

Althusser began to laugh giddily even as he limped and groaned.

Greenberg stumbled over a root and slammed down face first. The din of a rung bell echoed in his skull.

"Allons! Come on!"

His face felt crushed. His right eye had struck a root or stone. Rolling onto his back he raised a hand and tentatively touched his eye, hot and wet, his fingers slick with the oiliness of blood. He panicked. His imagination raced in all directions. He saw himself with dark glasses and a white cane, saw himself with a seeing eye dog, saw himself wandering, his arms out, lost in perpetual dark. He listed the great visually impaired people of history, Homer, Abe Lincoln, Cézanne, Aldous Huxley, Helen Keller, and of course Van Gogh who, with those yellow halos around everything, had to have been half blind.

"Greenbairg!"

"I'm blind."

"You will be dead too."

He tried to calm himself. Yet it was impossible, for without his vision he'd be more than blind; his very existence would be pointless; he was a visual creature; without his eyes he might as well be dead. And Rosenberg! Reeking of false sympathy—there, there, Clem, you can still listen to music—Rosenberg would visit him and offer to take him for walks. It was too gruesome to contemplate. Carefully opening the injured eye, a blur of black and grey swam and then resolved into a mesh of starlit branches. He groped to his hands and knees, white flashes pulsing behind the injured eye convincing him that his optic nerve was irrevocably frayed and bruised, and that he'd be plunged into a world of black and white, pencil drawings, a charcoal universe, the great Clement

Greenberg reduced to monochrome. He sobbed. Rosenberg had won. He may as well let Swen throw him in prison.

"Greenbairg!"

Jean Claude was standing over him. There were shouts in the distance. A gunshot. Or backfire. Greenberg staggered to his feet and hobbled on through the striped dark. "We have to go back for the car!"

"I told you, the car is lost."

They stumbled onward. The land began to descend and the trees thicken until they were forced to proceed single file. Soon the ground grew spongy and Greenberg smelled water and there, through the trees, gleamed a stream flowing black and silver in the moonlight. They halted on the muddy bank.

Squelching through mud, Jean Claude disappeared into the darkness leaving Greenberg and Althusser cowering. Had he abandoned them? Was it time for Greenberg to save himself? Then Jean Claude returned towing a skiff.

"There are no paddles," said Greenberg.

Jean Claude twisted a branch from a tree and said to get in. Greenberg and Althusser obeyed and Jean Claude shoved the boat out and clambered in and poled them into the current, which caught them in its momentum. Soon they were gliding swiftly. Using the branch as a tiller was unnecessary for the skiff stayed its course and in minutes the town, the tavern, Swen, and everything was behind them and there was only the night, the silence, and the stars.

Friday, 26 October, 1962

So you're bitter.

I guided Helen's brush stroke by stroke. Advised her on colour, form, everything.

Relationships are like fruit.

Fruit? What kind of fruit? What are you jabbering about? You're the fruit.

Yes, Clement, yes, vent your rage. But the simile holds. Fruit—the more you handle it the more it bruises.

I told her what to read. How to see.

We walk naked over glass.

Glass? I thought it was fruit.

The heart is an apple of blown glass, Clement.

Taught her how to think. Who to like. Who to sneer at. We were a couple. A team. Or so I thought. More fool me.

When we're in love we roll naked in the crushed glass of each other.

Rosenberg had his eye on her. He was jealous. He meddled. He always meddled.

The crushed glass of our—

Action Painting. What shit. What dreck. Artists knuckle-balling paint at the canvas. And then what does Helen do? What does she do? Marries Motherwell. Motherwell! An Action Painter! She might just as well have jumped in the sack with Rosenberg. Which she probably did.

Rumour, Clement.

No, not rumour. I saw the way they looked at each other. The way Rosenberg would come up behind her and lean down to say something and the way she'd smile.

What kind of smile?

What kind of smile do you think? An inviting smile. A smile that said more, give me more. Whenever I asked what the creep had been on about she'd get all airy and forgetful. It was Rosenberg. He did it. He broke us up.

Clement, Clement, Clement…love, friendship, intimacy, these things are never equal. We are tribes of one. Warring tribes. You invited Helen to your teepee and she stole your wampum.

❧

Long before dawn, they were shivering, the chill damp river air having leached the heat from their bodies. Althusser curled in his tweed jacket in the bottom of the boat muttering in French, sucking his thumb, then muttering some more, while black-sweatered Jean Claude hunched at his improvised tiller, and Greenberg hugged himself in his sport coat on the forward thwart, no idea in which direction they were headed but pretty sure it was the wrong one. It was now Friday morning and he was due in Emma Lake Monday. If he didn't make it he'd lose his thousand dollar stipend, lose the profile in *Canadian Art*, lose the near sexual joy of being listened to, of having people write down his words, ask him questions as though he was an oracle, gaze in admiration and envy upon the wonder of a man who had known Pollock, while Rosenberg would reign like a king, a thought that caused his back to spasm, his toe to throb, and his injured eye to twitch and pulse and blur. If he was condemned to wear an eye patch, would that repel or attract women?

Illuminated by starlight, the landscape was flat, but not without a desolate beauty: Munch without the scream. With dawn, fields took form and stretched away on either side in varying shades of brown and green; soon winter would set in and the land would freeze and the dominant colour would be grey. With the rising light, blurred shapes came into focus; images appeared, faded, then reappeared. He'd long believed that photography was inescapably literal, and film even more so. The masses expected it. Narrative. Give us narrative! But was it possible to watch a screen evolve through shapes and colours that were nothing but themselves, or to push further, to watch one colour, say, blue, a variety of blues, royal blue, sky blue, sapphire blue, robin's egg blue, silver blue, ocean blue, indigo, with a monologue overtop that addressed the theme of blue in all its permutations? He could imagine the letters he'd receive.

Greenberg received scores of letters each month. The range of people who'd read his work bemused and pleased him, from academics to housewives, to veterans of World War I and II who did watercolours of battlefields classical and modern.

Dear Mr Greenberg,

I am writing to you from the Netherlands, birthplace of paper. Many people think that the Chinese invented paper but that is wrong. Make no mistake, the Dutch invented paper as well as ink and most pigments as we understand them today. Flemish chemists formed an enclave in Florence in the twelfth century, where they plied their trade and also, by the way, invented spaghetti.

But these are not the reasons why I am writing you. I believe in efficiency, in getting a bang for your buck, and this cannot happen without accuracy. To wit: Abstract Expressionism. You claim it comes via Cubism whose main practitioners, Picasso and Braque, were Spanish and French. That may be. Who am I to judge? But I think you should know that Abstract Expressionism was invented by the Dutch. I direct you to the work of Geert van der Meer (1599 - 1650). And lest you conclude that he was an oddity, and not representative, see the paintings of Bootsma, Meyer, and of course Bent Baaker (1777 - 1855) who coincidentally wrote Confessions of a Dutch Opium Eater, as well as groundbreaking studies on plate tectonics, natural selection, and hygiene. In short, Bent Baaker is our da Vinci.

These facts and many more are well known to Dutch people, but we keep them under our hats so that we do not appear self-regarding. We are a humble folk. We cultivate our tulips and battle the sea. Toil is our lot. We labour after truth and accuracy, and it is in this spirit—the spirit of truth but also of forgiveness—that I write to you. I forgive you for your errors Mr. Greenberg, I forgive you.

Yours,
Hendrika De Groot

Dear Mr Greenburger,

I am an aspiring artiste confused about the future. It seems to me that there is a big fork in the road. Correction. It seems to me that there are many big forks in the road. There are forks, big and small, all over. The roads are full of forks! So my question, Mr Greenburger, is which fork to take? Not that I want you to tell me where to go. But maybe a hint. Or a tip. Like in the Daily Racing Form. (I work as a teller on weekends at Belmont. Do you like horse racing? I can get you in free through the employees' entrance. Anyway, let me know.) Right now I'm doing collages with old betting tickets. The tickets are all losers, of course, otherwise they wouldn't be lying all over the floor or in the bins. But I'm thinking that I'll include one winning ticket and that will be like the perfect flaw in the raku ware pot. (My older brother Gene did two years in Japan after the war.) Maybe I can show you some of my work. I could bring it by. Just say the word. Anyway, Clement—I hope you don't mind me calling you Clement— I've taken up enough of your valuable time.

Thank you,
Estelle Pinkman

Ah, Greenberg,

Sorry to bother. But then I'm in a perpetual bother. Botheration is my middle name. Point being, mate, I count myself bewildered vis your boy Pollock. In a bit of a quandary.

Adrift. At a loss. Allow me to set the scene: me in gallery. On gallery wall, a picture. Or rather let me rephrase: on gallery wall a painting. For there was nothing pictured, that is to say no image, no discernible reference to the quotidian. Nary a pansy or clipper ship or reclining nude in sight. Now leave me not be coy. I was not expecting pansies, clipper ships, or re-clining nudes. Was well aware of what I was getting into. Would have to live under a rug not to be hip to the Ab Art scene, man. And not being without a modicum of curiosity, I betook myself hence. Donned the roll neck sweater and Nehru jacket, gave the French toes a buff, and sallied forth to the Place des Artes.

And beheld.

It was, I admit, impressive. Even if Impressionism was not the mode. But the picture had presence, in spite of lacking eyes or face. I felt an animating spirit, an attitude, for yea, verily, I had come upon The Beast, and The Beast did laugh. My bewilderment was being mocked. It seemed that my ceil-ing was too low to achieve lift off. Epiphany denied. The REJECTED stamp slammed down. So I shut my eyes and counted to three and opened them again trying to fall into the epileptic élan of the thing, shuck the conventions, slough off the old skin and emerge anew, seeing and believing, buoyed on the wave of an epiphany, yes, an epiphanic moment, that is what I desired, gratitude beyond understanding.

Did I get this? No. Rather I got frustration. And if not for the timely interference of the guards, Reg and Hal, I'd have succeeded in tearing the thing from the wall and trampling it for what it was: the visual ravings of a drunk worth no more than a cockroach skittering about in pigment.

Nothing personal, you understand, everything is political.

Yours in the picture plane,

Hieronymus

❧

They'd joined a river, the narrow stream now three hundred yards across, each bank heavily outlined in dark mud as if drawn in black pastel. A flock of small birds flew past and Canada geese arrowed high overhead like the wake of a boat traveling the cold blue waters of a far off sea. One-eyed, Greenberg saw the river and the fields and the sky flattened to two dimensions, to surface, to a picture plane. This scene was given the seed of a narrative by the sun erupting on the horizon like the slow motion footage of a nuclear explosion. He was loathe to admit it now, but until the past few weeks, he'd always rather enjoyed the visuals associated with the bomb, had been able to ignore the devastation and focus on pure colour and form and motion, had discovered a fresh appreciation for the word *furl*, so smooth, so upward, the floral quality of a time-lapse mushroom as it rose and opened itself to the sky...

Jean Claude announced that they were traveling south-east.

"Back the way we came," said Greenberg.

"Back the way we came," agreed Jean Claude, poking at his cast which was disintegrating from its dunking in the river.

Althusser's ankle was twice normal size and Greenberg's brow pounded and his eye was hot and swollen as a soft-boiled egg. He mulled the advantages of a patch versus a glass eye. A patch could be rakish. There was mystery. Glass eyes looked eerie.

The river continued bending east. On a low bank stood a small house in an orchard silhouetted by the sun.

"We must go there," croaked Althusser.

Greenberg shielded his brow with one hand and pried open his swollen eye with the other. "Keep going."

"No," said Jean Claude, "he is right. We are too exposed out here."

"Just waltz up and knock on the door?" argued Greenberg. "Say, hi, we're on the run from the law, can we use your bathroom and by the way maybe borrow your car? That's not exposed?"

Jean Claude, ignoring him, steered them toward land.

⚬⚭⚬

The keel ground against the bank and they climbed out, each unable to avoid soaking his injured foot. Jean Claude's cast had by now completely fallen away exposing a swollen blue-black toe, but he limped briskly through the tall, dry grass that was still pale with the burnt tones of summer. Althusser dragged his ankle and muttered, while Greenberg's eye seeped. On either side of the path, blackberry bushes enmeshed the trunks of apple trees full of scabby fruit and hateful crows. The low sun lit the house and the night's mist lifted like a mood.

Jean Claude jutted his chin. "Go. Knock."

It wasn't much of a house, weathered clapboard in need of paint, one of the eavestroughs sagging, a broken window pane covered in cardboard. Greenberg warily mounted the worn wooden steps. On each sat a clay-potted rose, the flowers gone but the thorns sharp and hips reddening. The battered plank door had no window, while the dangling cut-glass doorknob was clearly salvaged from elsewhere. He knocked, lightly but firmly in what he hoped sounded innocent and neighbourly—shave and a haircut!—then stepped back and slid his hands into his trouser pockets and waited, marking time to the bump of his heartbeat. A minute passed. Then another. He knocked again. He leaned to see through the window, the glass as rippled as puddle ice. Nothing. He looked at Althusser and Jean Claude and shrugged.

Jean Claude led them around the house to a barn. When they entered, pigeons flapped and dust rolled in sun shafts illuminating two heavily rusted pickups, a Harley Davidson, a two-tone Studebaker, a small yellow tractor, and a Chevy Bel Air.

Jean Claude took a turn around the Chev.

"I would like to have violent sex in this car," said Althusser.

Greenberg and Jean Claude looked at him, then at each other, and for a moment it seemed they might actually laugh. Jean Claude found the hood latch. To Greenberg the motor looked like early Braque. To Jean Claude it looked functional. He tugged at a few hoses, peered, sniffed, nodded. "I think is good."

"What? Steal it?"

But before Jean Claude could respond they heard a voice outside, a familiar voice.

"Madeleine Morning Star as stately as the moon."

Swen.

They crept into a corner and buried themselves in hay.

"Have you been listening to the radio?" Swen's tone was one of polite enquiry and measured concern.

A burred female voice responded. "Not unless I choose to ruin my day from the get-go."

"That might well be wise, for the times they are a-tryin' and no mistake. Have you been down to the river this morning?"

"There a surprise washed up on the bank?"

"Three men of the fugitive variety availed themselves of Randal Cosgrove's skiff last night. The current being what it is I calculate they might well have reached your estate or even beyond."

"Last I heard Randal Cosgrove was a fugitive."

"He is a man given to lapses, yes. May I?"

The barn door ached open and a tall woman entered wearing a jean jacket and gumboots. Divot-like scars on her cheeks put Greenberg in mind of ritual scarification. Swen stepped in behind her followed by Bob who appeared to be wearing the exact same jumpsuit.

"I hope you start this car regularly," said Swen of the Studebaker. "Otherwise the works'll gum up."

"You in the market for an automobile, is that why you're here?"

"Oh, I have a car at the county's expense, thank you kindly. But I am a firm believer in the principle of maintenance. A well-oiled machine being a thing of beauty, if you get my drift." He approached, leaving Bob by the door angling his head about like a radar dish. "But these fugitives are funny ones. They could be nothing at all. Pair of Frenchmen and one New York Jew. I believe they are what you call urbane. And I confess that I am nonplussed at the nature of their game plan. Am I interrupting your busy schedule?"

"You know me. Go, go, go."

"Your shelter in good order, is it?"

"You really think bombs're about to start falling?"

"JFK and comrade Khrushchev talked this morning. Was all over the news. The Russians have demands and High Fidelity sounds like he wants to go down swinging. Those Latinos. Firecrackers one and all. What the situation wants, however, is a touch of Teutonic cool."

"So why're you wasting your time on the three stooges?"

"That is a good point. I have a hunch they are *agents provocateurs* pursuing nefarious ends. And Bob is in agreement."

Bob stood as bald as a mannequin by the door.

"In North Dakota?"

"Not so strange as it sounds what with our missile silos, uranium mines, and of course our Bolshevik neighbours to the north."

"What, the Canuckleheads are gonna invade?"

Swen grinned. "Well, not as such. But I can tell you that I am not alone in my concern. Hardware is moving north even as we speak. Last night there was a massive mobilization."

Bob walked past them toward a cellar door propped open on a stick and stared down. He stood a long time.

"Anything to report there Bobbo?"

"Zip."

Swen's tone grew subdued. "So, how are you and Wanda holding up?"

"Had some flooding in the spring," said Madeleine. "Fruit's got scab. Pump's broke. Everything's broke."

"We all miss Andy," said Swen with grave deference.

Madeleine stared into the dirt. "Yup. Wanda's never been the same."

After a moment of due silence, Swen said, "You ought to attend to that cellar. Doesn't do to be without a functioning shelter. I can send someone."

Madeleine spoke through a tight jaw. "I'll deal with it."

"It is merely an offer, Madeleine. No strings. You should also fumigate. Is it a dirt floor?"

"You know it is."

"Fire and fumigation. I can lend you a flamethrower. Fire purifies. Very effective."

"That's kind of you."

Bob went past them in his strange sliding stride and on out the barn door.

"Just where is he from?"

"Bob? I believe he is Swiss. But don't hold me to it. You will let me know if you see or hear anything."

"Is there a reward?"

"Oh there's always a reward of some sort. A favour earned is a favour returned." The glint of the rake flared in his eye. He moved toward the barn door and then turned and scanned the walls and loft and rafters one last time. "You take care of yourself Madeleine." And he went out.

Madeleine stood in the door looking after him. A car started up and moved off. When its sound had faded Madeleine turned. "You can come on out."

They emerged from the hay and stood like boys called before the principal.

Madeleine crossed her arms over her chest. She was as shapely as she was tall and long-eyed. "Visits from Swen do not bode well," she said.

"Forgive us," said Jean Claude. "We will not stay. But this river, where does it end up?"

"The Mouse?" She regarded Jean Claude with an appraising curiosity. "Over the border."

"Saskatchewan?"

"Manitoba."

"It does a U-turn?" said Greenberg.

"Down then up," she said. "But in that piddly little tub of yours you're looking at two maybe three days unless you get hold of a motor. Should've swiped something bigger. Just what're you guys running from?"

"Confusion," said Greenberg. "A mistake."

"A mistake. Right. A lot of people run from mistakes. This mistake involve killing anyone?"

"No!"

"Rob?"

"Things were said."

"Said. Such as?"

"Political things. In Smokey's."

"Small town tavern and you talk politics at a time like this…" She shook her head and looked around the barn as if for someone to share her amazement at such wanton foolishness. She had long black hair in a single braid that swayed with her dismay. Her gaze returned to her three visitors. She frowned and compressed her lips as she evaluated Althusser's ankle, Greenberg's eye, Jean Claude's toe. "You look a might roughed up."

⚯

She left them in the barn and returned with a pot of coffee and a stew of lean dark meat and wild rice, told them they could rest up but would have to be down the road as soon as night fell. To their surprise, relief, and then concern, she did not linger or ask any more questions, something Greenberg and Jean Claude dwelled upon and Althusser ignored.

"If we'd showed up out of the blue in my barn," speculated Greenberg.

"Can you imagine Greenbairg with a barn?" said Althusser, the absurdity returning the colour to his face and glint to his eye.

Jean Claude smiled and said nothing. He was looking at the door through which Madeleine had departed.

Did barn ownership signal something special in France? Am I too urbane? wondered Greenberg. Was it, in a way, a compliment, or did it imply the very opposite, that he was effete, narrow, incapable? A real man, a renaissance man, could shoe a horse, plough a field, fix a tractor, as well as remark upon Plato and compose an ode. He found it difficult to envision Althusser doing any of these things, yet knew that in fact the Frenchman had had an earthy upbringing in rural Algeria. How Greenberg hated being mocked. It felt that he'd spent his life creating an armour to protect himself, that his every review, article, and essay was another plate in that armour.

When they finished eating, they each found a place where the sun shone in through a crack. Althusser assumed the fetal position and immediately dozed off. His sleep was as chaotic as his waking, limbs twitching, mouth working, at one point reciting something stately in Latin, the only word Greenberg catching being a reference to death. *Mori* something. He'd had an uncle Morrie. In spite of his exhaustion, Greenberg could not succeed in escaping the glare of his own consciousness. He lay in the itchy hay and took stock. He was being pursued by the police, he was late for Emma Lake, he'd entered some murky conspiracy with an embittered French assassin, bombs were about to drop, the world end, and he was holed up in a North Dakota barn with a smashed eyeball and stomped toe. These were not good things, these were not his areas of expertise. What did he know from things nuclear? It had to do with breaking molecular bonds—or was it forging new ones? Atomic bombs and hydrogen bombs—were they different? There was fusion and fission, there was uranium and plutonium. Uranus and Pluto. Planets. Gods. Uranium was mined. But plutonium? Did it come from Pluto?

He sat up. Across from him, against a stall door, leaned a broom made of twigs, a spade, and a wooden pail whose staves were held by two metal straps while its handle was rope. Rustic Americana, a composition worthy of Grant Wood. That, that he knew something about. But radiation? Russians? He shut his eyes and recalled Johnson, the caretaker of a Bronx apartment building they'd lived in when he was a child. Johnson had newspaper pictures of Babe Ruth and Lou Gehrig tacked to his walls. Stiff-shouldered and bad-backed, pelvis brittle, spine curved, he shuffled like an amiable fiddler crab. Johnson was a nothing, a zero, a man who had accomplished zip, a broom pusher, a mop jockey, a plunger of toilets and emptier of trash bins who lived alone in a room by the boiler and yet was always grinning, always had a good story and a good word. He was a pigeon fancier whom Greenberg had often seen smiling beatifically as his birds hovered in a halo of cooing white angels. It was as if Johnson had been blessed with the divine gift of Christian grace, and at the moment Greenberg—who'd never wished to be a goy—envied it.

The sleeping Althusser began talking again. "Please Mr Omo, more broccoli s'il vous plaît!"

In the late afternoon Madeleine returned carrying a shotgun across the crook of her arm and aimed it at them.

"That is a very fine weapon," observed Jean Claude.

"Like guns, do you?"

"Not particularly."

"Me neither. Nonetheless they do come in handy on occasion."

"Is this an occasion?" asked Greenberg.

"Not yet. Though in my experience things do have an unfortunate tendency to change for the worse. Let's hope this isn't one."

Greenberg had the disconcerting experience of seeing himself from afar. There he was: writer, aesthete, avatar of high culture, the embodiment of sophistication, seated in the dirt of a barn with a shotgun aimed at him. "Has something changed? I mean, first your most generous hospitality and now—"

"I've been thinking."

"You want money?"

"I want a happy ending."

Althusser woke but did not sit up. "Shoot me. I don't care. I do not exist anyway. I have never existed. Not in any way that matters."

Madeleine regarded Althusser without expression or interest, as if she'd seen more than her share of idiots and intellectuals, then pointed the shotgun toward the door and said to Greenberg, "Swen said you're an expert on pictures. Well, I got some for you to look at."

"Is the shotgun necessary?"

"When I'm inviting three fugitives into my house I'm afraid it is. Up and at 'em cowboys. Come on. Time to earn your keep."

They filed out in time to see an exhausted sun sink itself into a couch of grey-gold cloud and watch long shadows of leafless trees grope arthritically over the field. The crows—had he ever seen so many crows as he had in the past few days—resumed their harassment like so many harpies who would see them cursed to oblivion.

Climbing the wooden steps they entered a kitchen where a tin kettle hissed on an old wood-burning stove while a bruise-coloured pipe rose through the slat wood ceiling. On a plank table, two places were set with plain white plates, a cup and saucer, a folded white cloth napkin and a silver fork and knife. The walls were bare but for shelves containing pots and pans, though by the far door hung a battered print of Sargent's *The Daughters of Edward Darley Boit*, four young girls in white frocks gazing from the luminous mists of childhood.

Madeleine led them on through the room and up a steep set of narrow stairs to a door, knocked, waited, and then entered. In the room a woman sat in a rocking chair by a window with a blanket over her lap.

Hands on her hips, Madeleine turned to look at the three men waiting on the landing. "This is my sister Wanda."

No one moved.

"Well," said Madeleine, "get on in here."

The ceiling sloped and the walls were papered in line drawings of mythic animals, hunters, rivers, trees, suns and moons, patterned and crosshatched with a mercurial sense of space that Greenberg found disorienting, as if the artist had no sense of up or down. The seated woman resembled Madeleine though was older, her grey-streaked black hair parted in the middle and hanging in two braids to her shoulders. Strewn on a trestle table were sheets of heavy gauge sketching paper as well as sticks of charcoal, pens, and dozens of pencils with teeth marks. There were newspapers as well, some yellowed, some recent. Greenberg's eye caught a headline: COUPLE ABDUCTED BY ALIENS. On the blanket in the woman's lap was a silver ball the size of a plum. Greenberg thought of Escher sitting in his room in the madhouse drawing his reflection in a glass globe. He looked from the drawings to the woman to Madeleine. What were they expecting, that he use his connections and curate a show for them, write an article, make her rich and famous?

"Interesting," he said, trying to sound positive.

"You best do better than that, Clem."

"What do you want? A show? I can make some calls."

The woman in the rocker did not seem to know they were there. She stared out the window over the darkening fields to the river where the skiff was tied.

"No calls, no shows," said Madeleine. "One of these pictures is a map that marks the location of a box."

Gazing at all the drawings, Greenberg thought of an IQ test. "What's in this box?"

"That's not your concern."

"But it could help," said Jean Claude, strategically.

Madeleine pushed out her jaw and considered. "Papers. A box yay by yay." Shotgun under her arm, she held out her hands indicating the size of a breadbox.

"And she knows where it's hidden?"

"I suspect so."

Greenberg was about to enquire why Madeleine did not

simply ask the woman where it was, when Madeleine added, "She hasn't talked in years."

"A map," said Greenberg.

"A clue," she said.

"And what, you think it's where, nearby, in the house or—"

"Somewhere on the property."

The colour was draining from the sky and gave the room a forlorn atmosphere. Madeleine put her hand under her sister's elbow and helped her stand. "Come on, Wanda. Supper." Wanda's hand grasped the silver metal ball in a tight fist, which she pressed to her chest and they went out of the room and down the stairs leaving the men to study the pictures, some years old judging by the curled corners and yellowed Scotch tape.

Althusser slumped into the rocker. "That woman has had electric shock treatment. I know. I can tell. It is there in her eyes. I had it in Sainte-Anne's. The technician he came to my bed carrying an organ grinder's box. Like so. With a crank. There were thirty of us. We would shout: Me first! Me first! We all watched him turn the handle that generated the charge. I would bite on a towel. I thought they were injecting my body with lightning. I could see the colour of my heartbeat. It hurt. I convulsed. But afterwards it was very good. I slept. My God, such a sleep..." He settled deeper into the chair as if trying to recapture the feeling.

Neither Greenberg nor Jean Claude commented. Instead, Greenberg pointed to a snaky shape with an asterisk for an eye. "It could be the river, and an island. Was there an island?" He went to the window but it was nearly dark.

"This one has a path and an x," said Jean Claude.

"They all have paths and x's," said Greenberg.

"But never a long enough sleep," said Althusser. "An hour and I was wide awake again in the white room of my mind."

All evening Greenberg and Jean Claude studied the drawings. They turned them over, they looked at them upside down. Madeleine, no longer carrying the gun, brought tea and ginger snaps. Greenberg said they were getting close and she called him a one-eyed liar.

"But it is obvious," said Althusser from the depths of the rocking chair where he had been dozing. Eyes closed, he said, "They are all the map. Follow any one of them and you will find the box." He twirled his wrist in a dismissive gesture as though it was facile. "They are like religion. They all lead to the same false god."

Greenberg removed a drawing from the wall and shoved it in Althusser's face. "Fine, then. Where is it? Where's the damn box?"

Not opening his eyes, he said, "The river."

"I've checked the river," said Madeleine.

"You must check again," said Althusser.

"Sure about that, are you?" Her tone was dismissive yet not altogether without hope.

"Very sure. The river." He sat up sniffing the aroma of Earl Grey. "Now I would like some tea and cookies."

"Why does she only have one?" Jean Claude asked Madeleine. "Of the balls. *Baoding* balls. You use two, and rotate them in your hand. Good for the chi. They use them all through the Orient," he explained. "They make a ting ting. Like chimes."

"Andy brought them back from Korea," she said. "I don't know what happened to the other one. Just like I don't know why he thought he had to go off to Vietnam." Before the moment could grow too awkward, she said, "Looks like you boys are going for a dip come morning. Better hit the hay."

☙❧

They returned to the barn where, surrounded by the rustle of mice, hunted by cops, haunted by Rosenberg, no car, no whisky, no cigarettes, Greenberg endured his ongoing insomnia while Althusser—sleep no longer evading him—snored resoundingly. Jean Claude as usual kept his distance. Greenberg imagined Jean Claude's years in Laos and Vietnam during the twilight of French imperialism, a twilight that had not been poetic or serene but ablaze with explosions and gunfire, kidnapping and murder, as it was now in Algeria—and as it could be any day now in Washington and New York—for apparently an American U-2 pilot had been shot down over eastern Cuba. This was too much. The game had changed and the gloves were off. The Americans—God's people—demanded a response. The Pentagon favoured taking out every missile site on the island and Greenberg, in spite of himself, soaring on the rapture of noble violence, could not help but agree and, exhilarated, imagined squadrons of B-52s flattening the whole place to a smouldering sandbar.

At the same time, he'd like to see it delayed a couple of months, even a couple of weeks, just long enough to deal with Rosenberg. Yes, let the world end but not before Rosenberg met his own end, not before he understood that he'd been defeated by the better man. After that, what did anything else matter? Well, a small voice observed, there was his son... A sting of remorse made him groan aloud, the same guilty pang that had accompanied thoughts of David ever since he was born.

Greenberg had been a happy dad. Behold, his offspring, a phenomenon, a creature, a miracle of the most primal order, not to mention proof of his virility. A went into B and boom, C, his son was born—with a little help from what's-her-name.

For a while the baby had brought them closer, for a while he'd actually been naive enough to think that they might make a go of it, but within months they began to drift, the little aggravations mounting, her impatience with his low earnings, her inability to appreciate the full arc of his destiny, her scarcely concealed mockery as he put Mozart on the RCA and set it next to the crib—the volume low—so that the child might absorb genius in his sleep.

Not that he wanted to make the child an artist, if such a thing were even possible. Greenberg knew more than enough artists—drunk, angry, envious, insecure, self-indulgent, self-pitying, self-aggrandizing—to ever nurture such qualities in his son. Yet that had been no reason not to give him pencils and crayons and paint and paper and say go to it. David had in fact shown promise. Perhaps they were accidents, but he did some surprisingly evocative sunflowers and a range of monsters with fearful, wondering, reflective expressions, as if these beasts were asking what it all meant, why had they been born? There were also episodes when David did not draw but stabbed the sketch pad until the pencil broke. There had also been a paper-ripping phase, during which he would lie in bed under a mound of shredded paper, holding each piece to his ear as though savouring a violin note and slowly, delicately, tweezing it into thin strips. Then again Greenberg had seen him hold a sheet of sturdy vellum up to the sunlight as though it was a screen through which to view an eclipse, except it was not an eclipse but an examination of the paper itself, a discovery of the fibrous terrain and cloud-like texture, dense here, fine there, as though the skin of the very firmament. To witness his son in a state of such bewonderment, so open to the world and his senses, had made Greenberg weep in joy.

David's mother, on the other hand, complained about the mess of paper, paper everywhere, paper torn, paper splotched, paper crumpled. It wasn't that she was superficial, she thought deeply about the state of her hair, her wardrobe, the table settings, the linen, the wall-to-wall, and no political scientist, no professor of comparative literature analyzed other women with such clear, hard, cruel subtlety. The question that remained such a mystery was what had drawn him to her in the first place. Her skin, yes, her hair, sure, her lips, of course, but perhaps most of all her inborn and inalienable membership in the inner circles and upper echelons of Westchester WASP-hood. An even more elusive question was what had drawn her to him? Why did she so willingly take her clothes off? Was he the means of a delayed adolescent rebellion? Was he a symbol? If so, of what? Social occasions were not easy. He'd not expected her to hold her own in discussions of art theory, but he could see in the flat matte of her grey eyes that unless it was upholstered with money and gilded with status, art and art theory was just so much rubbish and gibberish. He once asked her—perversely, ludicrously—what she thought was the appropriate art response to Mao and China and the millions of dead and she'd looked at him as if he was a talking toad.

How different she was from Helen. Helen…that trip to Paris. The galleries had been the least of it, meeting Althusser a mere aside, for nothing could compete with the view from the Hotel Palme d'Or over the rooftops. After a bit of amour-in-the-afternoon, they'd lie in the four poster gazing across the tiled slopes and the occasional whirl of pigeons—the light on their pearly underwings, the light on their powder-grey backs—watching the colours of the sky evolve and the lights come up, sharing the intimate whimsies of their brilliant minds, comparing signs from their prodigal childhoods, the chosen of The Chosen, and then, peckish, they'd descend in the caged elevator with its humming fly wheels and cables reminiscent of some Empire carnival ride, and greet the concierge knitting in her booth—dour old madame who had seen too much, two husbands, two wars—and stroll arm-in-arm beaming bonhomie toward a woman walking her siamese cat on a red leather leash, three school girls walking in step and laughing uproariously, a Moroccan in a knitted skullcap selling handbags on a corner, a woman in a fur with a nose like a hen, a man who could be Belmondo's twin lighting a cigarette as he departed a café. Paris. Voltaire, Balzac, Lautrec, de Beauvoir. The very dog-piss-and-cigarette-smoke smell of the place! On they went until they found a bistro, or a bistro found them. Oh God, why hadn't they died then and there!

Lying in that North Dakota barn, he put his face in his hands. His blanket smelled of horses. Horses rotting in ditches had been Johnson's dominant memory of World War I. The rest he declined to speak about. Maybe old Johnson had been wise in his own odd way. He was a good whistler, always toodling silly tunes. Greenberg's mouth was gluey, he needed a toothbrush, a hot shower, a Scotch, two Scotches, a whole bottle. At the moment he was inclined to think that hot water and Scotch were the two greatest accomplishments of the species. So much depended upon a glass of Johnnie Walker Red glazed with a little rainwater...it solved problems and soothed pain. And art? Art solved nothing. Though it might—might—salve pain of the existential variety. Though he'd have to think about that.

Is that what they needed now? Khrushchev had pulled the pin from the grenade and was holding it above the world's head, so what to do, look at a Pollock, listen to Mahler, read Proust? Maybe Kennedy, not an utterly soulless fool, was looking at Monet's bathers, that river scene with the row boats and the trees and the people in their old style bathing costumes, and thinking he ought to take Jackie and the kids to France—that is if there was a France left to take them to. Maybe Khrushchev was even now looking at Repin's Cossacks? And Fidel? Reading José Marti? Greenberg stared into the dark. As well as horses he smelled hay and dirt and manure and leather. They were good smells, the odours people had been living with intimately for thousands of years. His back hurt and his feet were cold and his eye ached. He'd never taken David to France. He hadn't seen him in what, ten months? Was it possible that so much time had passed without seeing his one and only son, without even thinking of him? He felt a tearing inside him, a fibrous ripping as if his soul was being torn into strips the way David had torn paper. He hung his head.

ॐ

Does he want to see you, Clement?

I don't know.

Does he call?

He used to.

Write?

Rarely. It's her fault. She kept us apart.

Ah, the excuse.

No, the explanation.

You blame her.

She punished me via him.

Did you fight to see him?

I tried.

Did you, Clement?

He grew distant. She worked on him. Told him stories. I could see it in his face. He looked at me like I was a stranger.

How did that make you feel?

Boy I hate that question.

Explore that question, Clement. Write about it. Or paint it.

Paint it?

You're the expert.

But not an artist. And don't dare ask me how that feels. If only—

Ah, if only.

If only Helen and I had had a son.

A different son? Or David?

The same son.

Is that possible, Clement? Listen to yourself.

Why? That's what I'm paying you for!

Saturday, 27 October, 1962

"Greenbairg."

Cool air on his eyeballs—evidence, in spite of the dark, that both his eyes were open.

"Do you know why I did it?" Althusser's voice reaching him from out of the night. "Do you know why I killed her?"

Greenberg stayed very still, as if a predator was circling.

"Have you ever tortured a dog?"

Swallowing, he said, "I killed a goose."

"Did you eat it?"

"No."

"That is a waste. I do not hate the Germans. I did not hate the camp. It was steady. It had a routine. The food, well… But why would you kill a goose?"

"I don't know…I just…to look death in the face."

"And what did death's face look like?"

"I couldn't look. I turned away at the last moment."

"How small she looked, my Hélène. How uncomfortable she seemed half on and half off the bed. Her pelvis twisted,

her mouth open, the tip of her tongue dark pink. Someone—
I cannot recall that it was me but then I cannot deny it
either—had draped the old red curtain across her like a sash.
I thought of victory, I thought of blood, I thought of France,
la gloire... She was wearing her nightgown, white with blue.
I said, 'Hélène...Hélène...' She did not answer and I understood what I had done, so I ran out of the room shouting I
have killed my wife! I have killed my wife! Oh God! Oh God!
Somewhere someone was singing in Arabic. I knew the song.
I had heard it many times as a boy, a song about the harmat-
tan, the wind that carries madness. She had a fine voice, this
woman singing in Arabic, low and melodious and yet coarse,
like sea salt, like sand sifting through flowers. Greenbairg, I
never hit her. You must believe me. Ask our friends, our colleagues, our neighbours, never was I violent. We argued, yes.
She created scenes, yes. I two-timed her, yes. I will tell you a
secret: I never kissed a woman until I was thirty. Not until I
was twenty-seven did I masturbate."

Greenberg waited for him to go on, intrigued, appalled.
The dark had begun slipping away as silently as an outgoing
tide. Jean Claude was now visible standing at the barn door
looking at the dawn. Horse blanket around his shoulders, he
put Greenberg in mind of a shaman, a man who communed
with the dawn and the dusk. His back was to them. Without
turning, Jean Claude asked, "Louis. You still have not explained why you did it."

"Why? Because she wanted me too much. I always go into
the hospital when women declare their love. Every time. I feel
safe in the hospital. Protected. In the hospital I have a wise
and caring father—the doctor—and a sweet and loving
mother—the nurse."

"Little Louis," said Jean Claude, not utterly without af-
fection.

"Oui, petit Louis."

"They say you are impotent," said Jean Claude.

"No. I have phimosis. My foreskin, it is too tight."

"Your little man's hat is too small," said Jean Claude. "You should cut it off."

"And you should have joined the communists. She would be alive."

Three strides and Jean Claude loomed over Althusser.

Althusser turned his face upward as if exposing his breast to a sword. "Kick me if it will make you feel better. But remember, the greatest will to power is the strength of will not to take power."

Jean Claude was weeping. The light was widening the barn by the second, shaping out corners, clarifying colours, raising the ceiling as though the lights were coming up on a stage. "Do you never shut up?"

"No, I never learned how to ferme my *bouche*. I am Latin. I give in. It is why Santayana left this Protestant US of A and returned to Spain, so he could be with people who gave in to their passions."

Jean Claude, baffled, raised his arms and let them drop.

A pitched shriek tore the air.

Running outside, they saw a formation of three jets streaking toward the sunrise, contrails chalking the vermilion sky.

"And so it begins," intoned Althusser.

"No," said Jean Claude, "so it ends." He looked around as if expecting troops to come running at them from the woods, but there were only the trees and the fields, even the crows were silent. Propping his foot on a round of wood he studied his injured toe.

"Jews don't have that problem," said Greenberg.

Althusser and Jean Claude looked at him. Greenberg saw their confusion. "Phimosis," he said.

"Yes," said Jean Claude. "You should convert, Louis. Go to the mohel. Have it cut off. Be free."

"Free?" Althusser spoke wonderingly. "That is exactly why I killed her. To be free."

"Then you are happy." But Jean Claude's voice was drained. He swallowed drily.

Althusser was about to respond, but Madeleine appeared striding toward them through the dead grass. Behind her the sun hung trembling beyond the river. Her shotgun rode the crook of her elbow like a pet.

"What's the news?" Greenberg asked her, nodding to the sky where bands of vapour had begun to drift and fade.

"Got more important things on my mind than Armageddon, Clem. As should you." She escorted them down the gently sloping field to the river. "Go to it, boys."

It was not an inviting prospect. The water looked like cold steel.

Jean Claude pried off his one shoe, pulled down his trousers, shook them, folded them, lay them over a log, removed his jacket and shirt. He was still tanned from the summer and had a tattoo of the *fleur-de-lis* on his right bicep. Wearing only pale blue boxers, he waded into the icy water that coiled itself around his legs. When he reached mid-thigh, he went into a crouch and, shielding his eyes against the chill light glancing off the surface, peered into the swirling river. He plunged his arm in up to the shoulder, the movement so sudden that for a moment Greenberg thought Jean Claude had been caught by a snare or worse and was about to be dragged under. Doubled over, head twisted to one side, Jean Claude frowned as though listening to submerged sounds, then abruptly stood straight and shook water from his arm. The next quarter hour went like this, Jean Claude up to his chest, moving upriver, downriver, deeper, shallower, pausing, reaching, at one point submerging himself entirely. He found three beer bottles, a length of rebar, a bicycle.

Madeleine paced the riverbank with her shotgun. She wore her felt-lined denim jacket, a thick grey sweater, jeans and gumboots. Halting, she whirled on Greenberg and Althusser. "Why's he doin' all the work? Get on in!"

"You are very beautiful," crooned Althusser, limping toward her in what he seemed to think was a suave manner.

She regarded him as though he was some sort of salamander.

Greenberg removed his slacks and shoes and waded into the skin-shrivelling water. It crept up his legs and over his knees and advanced up his thighs to his groin and shrank his scrotum. He halted, jaw clenched and neck so tight he feared there would be damage to his vocal chords. The day after tomorrow he was scheduled to deliver the keynote speech at Emma Lake, a speech he'd spent a week composing, a speech that was in his suitcase in the Dodge. Rosenberg would have to step in. The bastard was probably having breakfast at the moment, buttering a bagel, adding some compote, or lox, a few capers and sliced onion, sipping coffee, knuckling crumbs from that obscene moustache, and expressing a deep and bewildered concern over Greenberg's absence while offering the discreet observation that old Clem was, well, under a lot of stress and who knew if such events weren't just a little beyond him now…

He scooped water and scrubbed his face. It felt good on his eye. The swelling had eased and he could see his reflection wobbling in the current. A glance at Madeleine—stern, unbending, impatient—told him that unless they found this box they'd not be getting anymore hospitality and certainly no ride to the border, that more than likely they'd be back in the skiff floating downriver, that is if Madeleine didn't call Swen.

Greenberg called to Althusser, "You're sure about this?"

"I am sure about nothing." He was seated cross-legged in the tall grass, resembling some woeful holy man who had lost faith.

"But—" There was no point reminding him that he'd said it was obviously in the river.

Instead, Greenberg moved downriver from Jean Claude and began squinting into the water, which ran like a close-up in a film, free of signs and referents, plot and character, nothing but colour and motion. In other circumstances, he might well have been inspired. He must remember this: the river, transitory and cruel, flowing and yet still, the water yielding yet treacherous, and here, now, opaque, defying all attempts to plumb its secrets. Still, he went after those secrets. He reached in, the frigid water shocking his ribs and armpit so that it was all he could do not to yelp. Nothing. He found nothing. Althusser was playing them for chumps. He tried again, and again, and was about to give up when his foot struck a stone causing him to cry out, flail his arms and pitch chin first into the river. He paddled and wallowed, opening his eyes long enough to see a black box, and emerged coughing but shouting as well. He plunged back under. The box wasn't big, but it was weighty. Fighting the current, losing his footing, cursing in frustration, his submerged voice roiling alien in his ears, he got the box to the surface only to discover that it was chained.

He held it over his head showing the others, straining, victorious, seeing himself for an instant as Hercules accomplishing one of his labours.

Madeleine wasn't as happy as he thought she'd be. In fact she sounded frustrated. "Shit."

Greenberg felt indignant. Had he not found the treasure? He was about to complain when he heard a motor.

"Dump it and hide," she said through stiff lips.

Greenberg dropped the box and wading up out of the river grabbed his pants and shoes and hid in the grass.

The boat was still tiny but its motor was growing louder with furious purpose. As it came arcing in, Jean Claude, still in the water, turned to face it. Madeleine stood firm. Althusser had vanished. The hull scraped the bank and the wake surged up washing away Greenberg's footprints while threatening to swamp Jean Claude. NORTH DAKOTA STATE POLICE was printed in large black letters on the white hull. Two men in uniform leaned on the windshield, one in his forties and the other in his twenties, both wearing crew cuts and indigo coats with gold badges.

"Kind of late in the season for swimming," said the older one.

"It's called a baptism," said Madeleine. "Know what's good for you you'll get yourself in that water, too."

"Preacher, are you?"

Madeleine opened her arms wide in a gesture that might have been an act of benediction.

The younger man almost laughed scornfully but contained himself and looked to the older man who, of a more cautious and respectful nature, pushed up the bill of his indigo cap. "That your skiff?"

"It is."

"Live here, do you?"

"About ten thousand years."

The older man chose to ignore the implications. He looked at Jean Claude who had pulled on his pants and shirt. "Feel cleansed, do you?"

"As the driven snow," he said in a precise American accent. As casually as possible he worked his feet into the sand to conceal his injured toe.

The man studied Jean Claude. "We're looking for three men."

As he spoke another trio of jets arced south-east across the sky.

"We at war?" asked Madeleine.

"Should be," spouted the younger man.

"Eric," warned the elder.

"Well." He spat into the water.

"Calling it Black Saturday," said the older man. "One of ours dead. Say Khrushchev was eating caviar and drinking vodka to celebrate. Then that business this morning."

"What business?"

"You didn't hear?"

Madeleine waited.

"Radar station configured to detect missile launches from Cuba thought it had a hot one. Whole eastern seaboard nearly crapped. Mistook a satellite for a nuke. Came that close to launching an all-out counter attack."

"Ask me they still should," said Eric.

"Quite the little chicken hawk you got there," said Madeleine.

Eric seemed unsure as to whether he was being mocked or praised. The older man surveyed the scene once more, eyes narrowed more in an expression of general interest in the landscape than a search for suspects. Finally, he nodded. "See any strange activity, you call the authorities."

"I will."

The man touched his cap in salute, put the boat in reverse, drew off, then gunned his way downriver. When the boat was gone and the wake had settled, Jean Claude waded out, submerged himself and retrieved the tar-coated box. Braced against the current, he held the box in one arm and tried the bolt in the shackle; it turned easily, the threads still thick with grease.

༺༻

In the kitchen, Madeleine clunked down a red metal tool case on the table beside the box, flipped up the catch and lifted the lid. Tiered shelves opened out revealing an impressively organized array of implements for Jean Claude to sort through until he found the screwdriver he wanted.

Wanda was seated at the end of the table with the Baoding ball in the middle of her plate as though it was some exotic confection. A tin kettle approaching a boil began trembling on the stove. Greenberg stood as close to the heat as he could without setting his clothes on fire. Hugging his hands in his armpits he trembled and burned, skin hot, insides ice, clenching his teeth so tightly he feared for his dental work. Perhaps it was the cold affecting his brain, but he was convinced that the black box contained some malevolence. Hypothermic hallucinations? He rarely hallucinated. Even the time he and Pollock ate peyote he'd seen no visions or colours, got only gut knotting cramps followed by eight hours of melancholy while Pollock painted the air with his penis.

Madeleine arranged a blanket across Jean Claude's shoulders as he carved away the tar with the screwdriver until he'd exposed a padlock. Selecting a pipe wrench, he was about to twist the lock off when he looked at Madeleine and offered her the honour. Her confidence seemed to abandon her and she breathed with difficulty. Wanda sat very still though her glance flicked from the box to Madeleine and back to the box. Madeleine reached out slowly and took the wrench, turned the screw adjusting the jaws, then clamped them to the padlock and, getting a nod from Jean Claude, firmed her grip and compressed her mouth and with both fists cranked the wrench. The padlock held but the latch broke exposing pale splintered wood. Using both hands she tried separating the tar-sealed halves. They clung.

Then exploded.

Everyone fell back. Wanda threw herself to one side uttering a croak. Shielding his face, Greenberg hit the floor in the fetal position. After a full minute, as though by common consent, they all lowered their arms and stared at the grinning clown head that bobbed and wobbled on the end of the coiled spring. Althusser gurgled gleefully as if he was behind the prank. He cupped the clown's head as though it was a lolling rose. Ignoring the clown, Madeleine peered cautiously into the box and came out with a plastic sleeve containing documents. She also found a metal ball.

"Andy." Wanda's voice was slow and otherworldly, like the first word of a wakened sleeper. She reached across the table and Madeleine set the ball in her hand and Wanda sat back holding the two balls, one in each fist, to her breast. Madeleine opened the plastic sleeve and undid the lace on a grey folder.

"Is it what you wanted?" asked Jean Claude.

She didn't answer at first. She read. Then nodded. "The powers that be said we didn't have title. No records. Well, now we got them."

"He is a fine little fellow," said Althusser of the clown. It had a chalk-white face, red hair, thick red lips and a gaping mouth with a long red leather tongue, the eyes marbles with yellow cat's eye pupils.

"Andy had a sense of humour," said Madeleine.

They heard a tinkling sound, like small wind chimes in a light breeze, and discovered Wanda absorbed in rolling the two metal balls around and around in the palm of her right hand.

❦

The mood of celebration was brief. All day the radio reported grim developments. Announcers ran out of adjectives: nerves were frayed, on edge, brittle, tense, taut, world peace hung by a thread, was in the balance, had reached the breaking point, Hiroshima and Nagasaki were mere blips compared to what loomed, until once again they wheeled out the Big Bertha of terms: Armaggedon. The army, navy, and air force had all been mobilized and the generals were meeting. The Pentagon was on code red. Helicopters and Grumman S2Fs were dropping sonobuoys and triangulating the echoes to hunt Soviet subs. The shadow of apocalypse was upon them.

Night seemed to come early and yet time slowed, the clock on the wall silent and the small advance of its second hand all that much more torturous. Conversation started, then stopped; was animated, then leaden. Sitting around the table, they fed the stove and drank coffee as Wanda's Baoding balls chimed.

Greenberg envisioned the future: a New York City reduced to ruins meant no galleries, no studios, no ateliers or salons, no art at all, leaving only traumatized survivors too stunned to do anything other than raise their charred hands and wail. He saw himself stepping through smouldering wreckage, past smoking stone and crumbled brick, skirting Daliesque distortions of melted glass and studying the grisly sculptures of twisted metal, a burlesque of man's creative endeavour. All that he'd lived for destroyed and, perhaps worse, the spirit of play crushed from the human soul. He looked at the others. Jean Claude appeared equally troubled, though excited as well, for even on the final day of the world the prospect of love persisted: he had his eye on Madeleine and she did not seem utterly averse. Althusser, meanwhile, was talking to himself, alternately grimacing and smirking as if performing all roles in a play. "On whose side is history?" he asked aloud as though addressing the audience, and then hiccuped with laughter. Greenberg spotted a beetle scurrying across the floor. It had an impressively black and glossy carapace. He repeated the word *carapace*, fondling its sharp but slippery sound: *carapace*. If the bombs dropped, would bugs inherit the earth? An earth reduced to a blindly spinning ball of mud twitching with insects, as devoid of imagination as the brutish Russians and the faceless Chinese with their posters of thick-wristed babushkas and clone-eyed drones clad in the same drab grey—couture always the first casualty of socialism—or might a Kandinsky or a Bulgakov survive to ring the bell in the coffin?

So it was all coming down, the future collapsing like a rotten house. What was David doing at this moment: pacing in a panic or obliviously idling? Greenberg's son had always been a mystery. For the past year, David had been living in a cabin in Maine, beavering away making candles, collecting wax, rolling it out, pouring it in angel moulds, in moulds of Beethoven's head, Jesus' head, Marilyn Monroe's torso. David's shack had become the chapel of some fire-worshipping hermit with candles lining every shelf, table, countertop, the backs of chairs, even the floor in various patterns hiding a Kabbalah whose key was known to him alone. Greenberg had visited once. His son, unwashed, unshaved, eyes of an old man reflecting the dance of flame and shadow on the stark walls. There were no pictures anywhere and the only books other than a copy of *The Sound and the Fury* were by Lobsang Rampa. Greenberg had picked up the Faulkner and discovered that the pages had been cut out and a wax crucifix inserted. In other circumstances he might have shown more appreciation of the craftsmanship, David's detailing of the figure on the cross gruesomely evocative.

If bombs did start dropping how would the boy cope? Boy? He was a man. Except in Greenberg's heart of hearts he'd always be a child—his child. He recalled standing with him in his arms on a ferry, and how the horn had sounded and

David, all of three years old, had flinched in fear and Greenberg had held him and felt his panicked breathing and racing heart against his own chest. How happy Greenberg had been to be there for him, how curiously fulfilled as he gazed past his child's fragrant head out to sea.

Sunday, 28 October, 1962

It was my decade.

The clock belongs to no man, Clement.

Abstract Expressionism. I recognized it. I nurtured it.

Chronos was the god of time.

And Rosenberg tried stealing it.

Prometheus stole from the gods and was punished.

Rosenberg should be punished.

Calling down vengeance is the job of gods and kings and judges. You would do better to learn from Rosenberg.

Learn? Learn what? How to backstab?

Rosenberg enjoys himself, Clement. He delights in the joust. He lives in time instead of lamenting in eternity. That is what you could learn from him.

I want him to die!

Clement. The mountaintop is a lonely spot. To whom will you sing? For whom will you dance? The firmament?

If I could paint or compose music then I'd do it. That would be a better vengeance on him, on all of them.

Then do it.

Don't you listen? The muse is fickle, a madwoman! It's not the deserving who get the talent!

꧁꧂

He woke on his side on the floor near the stove, his first sensation that of heat on his back, the second that his mouth was dry and sour, the third that the ting-tinging of Wanda's metal balls was gone, though the radio, lower now, continued the murmur of missiles.

Althusser lay nearby under the kitchen table while Jean Claude and Madeleine were notably absent. Greenberg squirmed closer to the stove—the coals ticking and popping— and drowsed back to sleep and dreamed of Independence Day fireworks exploding with red, white, and blue streamers arcing into the sky and then back down to earth, except they were not fireworks but missiles, the Russians and the Cubans and the Chinese ganging up on them. What a waste of human history. It was the triumph of representation. Soviet Realism— burly forearmed women wielding the hammer and sickle. What did that leave? Draughtsmanship? Bring on the potatoes and the cabbage soup and the shared poverty of the soul. He heard shrieks and cries and thought yes, here it is, the end, but woke not to Armageddon but to Madeleine and Jean Claude and Wanda embracing and chattering. Greenberg sat up and stared at the spectacle of Jean Claude—Jean Claude!— lighthearted and laughing.

Kennedy and Khrushchev had come to terms, the Russians were pulling out of Cuba and taking their missiles with them in exchange for an American promise not to invade. From the radio came the sounds of cheering crowds from cities across the country, and in a choked voice the anchorman spoke of great statesmen, Pericles, Hadrian, Lincoln, Churchill, and now Kennedy. Althusser made a performance of yawning, but even he could not completely mask his relief at seeing the dawn of another day. It was as though a hurricane had passed and they were watching its black and roiling mass dissipate in the distance.

They went out onto the porch to watch the sun emerge from the mist on the river. There was a faint scent of wild roses and cool earth and damp air. The sunrise was slow and transcendent in its ageless routine, and above all, gloriously immune.

Monday, 29 October, 1962

Madeleine let them off at a trail around midnight and said they were nine miles from the border. She gave Greenberg a bottle of homemade liquor and Althusser the clown from the box. Both men were moved. They held their gifts awkwardly in both hands before each stashed his prize inside his coat.

Reluctant to part, Madeleine and Jean Claude walked a little on their own holding hands, heads close, whispering, before she got back into the Chevy and drove slowly away while he stood on the roadside until the taillights were gone and the silence had resumed. After a suitable interval, the others joined him and Althusser suggested a toast. Greenberg had a corkscrew on his key ring and opened the bottle and they all took a drink of the hooch, some distillation of herbs and fruit and corn. They took stock. The earth was already whiskered in frost, no lights were visible in any direction, the air was icy, the sky clear, the constellations a familiar glitter.

"Well then," said Greenberg.

"After you," Althusser said to Jean Claude.

They proceeded in silent single file, Greenberg wondering if he could possibly reach Emma Lake by evening and salvage some of his residency. Surely they could reschedule his lecture, he could reassemble his notes from memory. There'd nearly been a nuclear war for God's sake!

They hiked all night and crested a hill just as the rising sun pressed itself into a ceiling of cloud and a blizzard struck like locusts. Althusser tore up fists full of grass and stuffed them inside his coat as insulation. Jean Claude put his head down and ploughed on while Greenberg fought not to guzzle the remainder of the booze. And yet in minutes, the blizzard swept over them and the sun reappeared and the ground looked like crushed white glass. They halted and watched the clouds travel off as if on a migration leaving behind a sky scoured blue.

"Can you feel it?"

They looked at Althusser.

"Feel what?"

"The air," whispered Louis. "We have crossed the border, we have left the Imperium."

The town of Ross was a stretch of nubbly tarmac, a gas station, a café, and a few wind-beaten buildings that seemed never to have recovered from the Depression. There was no railroad station, no grain silo, no highway, only a small wooden church of indeterminate denomination, the steeple thick with pigeons that rose and flapped when the wind gusted and then resettled themselves. Outside a liquor store, Greenberg, Jean Claude, and Althusser went into a huddle and pooled their cash. Between them they had two hundred and sixty-nine dollars. They entered the Prince of Wales Cafe and General Store—the sign dangling from rusted hooks and the hand-painted letters worn to the wood. The café smelled of dust and the woman behind the counter said, with a grim satisfaction that bespoke the dark glory of deprivation, that no bus stopped there, though one Wednesday a month a truck came through to fill the gas station's tank and they might catch a ride but that would mean waiting three weeks because the truck had just been. She was perhaps forty and had a Scottish accent, a vaguely freckled face, greying red hair, little or no neck, and wore a frock that may once have been patterned with daisies and a cardigan that resembled burlap.

"Could we pay someone to drive us to Weyburn?" asked Greenberg.

She drew her head back and raised her chin and regarded Greenberg through eyes used to facing gritty prairie wind. Her complexion beneath the freckles resembled tinned meat, and he imagined her entire face sliding out of a can. He saw her as Wyeth might render her: the round head that managed to be both fat and gaunt, the suspicious eyes, the hair a form of static electricity, her face a testament to disappointment, failed hope, deflated dreams, bankruptcy, abandonment, the ravages of wind, snow, flood, mosquitoes, disease, and crushing years of disheartening drought. Behind her on the shelves stood rows of Campbell's soup tins.

A young man pushed through a swing door connecting to the kitchen. Their faces made the family connection unmistakable. A big kid, husky, eyes small and suspicious. He looked at the strangers and then at his mother wondering what to do and whether violence was called for.

"They want to go to Weyburn," she told him.

She may as well have said Tibet.

He shrugged and returned to the kitchen.

They asked for coffee then retreated to a worn plywood booth. The coffee arrived in chipped white cups and tasted of dust. They drank in silence and accepted refills with gratitude. Warmed, they looked around the café with its tinned food, its boxes of Sunny Boy Cereal, Red Rose tea, storm candles, tins of lamp oil, the framed black and white photo of the young Queen Elizabeth, and then looked out the window. The glaze of snow glittered with an optimism unsuited to the moment. Down the street sat an old Packard—a late-forties model, grey with white wall tires—with a "4 Sale" sign.

❦

They reached the outskirts of Weyburn by early afternoon, the car swimming on its springs and flowing over the terrain like a boat on a slowly rolling sea. Jean Claude drove, with Althusser next to him and Greenberg in back trying not to obsess over the hole in the floor and the road streaming past only inches beneath his feet. He leaned his head out the window into the pummelling air so as to avoid inhaling the exhaust being suctioned up into the vehicle. A one-eyed man had demanded sixty-five dollars for the car. He'd removed rolls of chicken wire and old issues of *National Geographic* and a majestic set of moose antlers that had taken up the entire back seat. Good luck, he'd told them.

"Luck and goodness rarely travel together."

The man had stared at Althusser out of his functioning eye-ball, then stepped back into his yard and shut the gate and gripped it firmly as if prepared to defend his territory.

Althusser grew cheerier the closer they got to Weyburn. "The asylum is a place of order and repose, it is the eye of the hurricane, a place to be still. Have you ever been, Greenbairg?"

"No."

"No? But you must come. Both of you! We will all go together. We will convalesce. It is like a spa. They will give us robes, a bath, we will take our leisure. And together we will have electric shock. One for all, all for one." He kissed his bunched fingertips. "It is better than opium because it does not stop you from shitting. Do you like to shit, Greenbairg?" Althusser had turned almost fully around in the front seat. His face had lost its lines and his eyes had grown innocent with enthusiasm.

Greenberg admitted that it was one of the few reliable pleasures.

Althusser slapped the seat back. "Of course! And yet we don't speak of it, we deny it. This is wrong. This is unhealthy. Do you know that in India they refuse to even look at shit. Not even their own! They believe that it dirties the soul. This is madness. Jean Claude, are you with us?"

"Louis, I don't like hospitals."

"But you like to shit."

Jean Claude indulged him. He spoke softly. "Yes."

Having won the point, Althusser was gracious enough not to gloat. "You have been quiet, my friend."

"*Je suis fatigué.*"

"*Mais oui.* We have struggled. And now it is the end. We will part."

"Let us drive a little," suggested Jean Claude, catching Greenberg's gaze in the mirror; Greenberg looked away. He didn't have the jam to con Louis into killing Rosenberg. What had he been thnking? No, let him go get his electro-shock and his LSD. But what about Jean Claude?

Weyburn was small. Jean Claude made a right turn, then another, passing brick houses with tiny windows and short chimneys, and soon they were on a dirt road running through barren fields that would soon freeze solid for the next five months. They drove in silence beneath a vast sky that arched over the land. The wind bore an Arctic chill. Canada. Such a hollow word. Such a cold hard word. What sort of life was possible in a place so grey and vague and half-formed? Greenberg once drove his father's Buick to Montreal, a different Canada altogether. He'd had a good time, spoke French in a bistro with a waitress who met him afterwards and let him feel her up in a park where shrubs were flowering. He drove out to Quebec City—the only walled city in North America—and gazed upon the Plains of Abraham. Yet he felt guilty because his father—haunted by the uncertainties of Poland—

worried that his son was lost, spoiled, a wastrel, not under-standing that travel was research, or that an entire day spent lying in bed smoking cigarettes and reading everything from novels to poetry to philosophy was not laziness but study, growth, evolution.

When he got two stories—his only two forays into fic-tion—published by *Esquire* the old man changed his tune and offered him a hundred a month if he'd keep writing and go back to his wife and son. This had been an enormous capitu-lation, for his father had disapproved of him marrying *out* and had scarcely acknowledged David, his own grandson, something for which Greenberg would never forgive him. He and his father had rarely been close even though the family lived under the spell of Yiddish. As Greenberg hit adolescence and spent more time exploring English literature the spell was broken and the distance widened, for he was sailing off to other lands on the words of Joyce, Woolf, Hemingway, Fitzgerald, and Faulkner. They were his spiritual family, his true siblings. Yet having limited talent himself as a novelist or painter or musician he understood that his role was to be a hierophant; he would unlock secrets, reveal mysteries, illumi-nate, elevate, delight, for he believed in himself, quietly, doggedly, at time perhaps selfishly, because no one else did, and because there was no room for the faint-hearted in the arena of the soul, no time for the uncommitted, no patience with men unwilling to devote their lives to art, the only act that did not merely validate but exalt existence, the only act that made him able to bear both the world and himself.

His right eye was still sore. Looking out the car window he saw only a flat field of colour and shape, not a tree or building or person anywhere. Prairie. A lonely word. It lacked the romance of *steppe* because it lacked its Chekov or Gogol, or if it had one he'd not heard of them. Here, now, he saw only scrubby grass bending beneath an invisible wind. You could feel wind, smell wind, hear wind, observe its effect, harness its power, but never actually see it.

They spooked a murder of crows that fled uttering their death-land curses. Is that what Van Gogh heard when he painted them, the voice of death? This reawakened him to the deed about to take place. Dread spasmed his gut. Was Jean Claude really going to do it? Was Greenberg going to watch? Certainly he was aiding and abetting. Would he be repatriated to face the death penalty, spend his life on the run, and if not on the run then be dogged by guilt? How tired he was. He looked at Jean Claude whose jaw was tense. Greenberg's throat felt like rope and his temples throbbed while Althusser's neck was two frail cords of muscle beneath the exposed scalp. Scalp. What a bare and terrifying word.

Althusser began a low fond chuckle that grew louder. "Have I told you that I met the King of Dahomey?"

Greenberg was grateful for the diversion. "Tell us, Louis."

"A big man. Not one of our French runts, no. Tall, very tall, with broad shoulders. A proud man, a king, with a great calm about him. Every day he would walk the promenade in Algiers. He carried a cane with the skull of a cobra on top. And he wore a suit of gold cloth with ebony buttons. He had two small dogs on a red silk cord. He was in exile, you see. He had been deposed, but he would return, of that he was certain, for he had two lionesses that were pining for him, Greta and Garbo. His agents gave him reports. He became sad when he spoke of his lions. His mind had broken, but his dignity remained unvanquished. He would say to me, 'Louis, if you lose your dignity you are a worm.'"

The rumble of the tires over the frozen dirt counterpointed Althusser's nostalgia. Fields flowed past. The land was not so much defeated as waiting. All the windows were down to vent the exhaust flowing up through the floor. How we poison ourselves with our machines, thought Greenberg, giving in to a shameless romanticism, how much more stately life must have been before internal combustion—slower and yet richer and more intimate as they gathered in the salons lit by candles and heated by wood, to talk, banter, recite, sing, act, entertain, drink wine, and of course slip away to the curtained alcoves...what would Cézanne have thought of Vorticism, Futurism, Suprematism, Constructivism. Were these things art or engineering?

More immediately, did Jean Claude plan to stab Althusser or slit his throat? Or did he mean to strangle him? He hoped Jean Claude could do the deed swiftly and painlessly, and out of sight. Poor mad Louis, his soul bleeding like so much air from a child's balloon.

They pulled over by the remnants of a shed. The cooling engine ticked in the wind.

Jean Claude got out, his door squawking on its dry hinge, and walked to the shed, which was little more than two walls and a collapsed roof, a length of fencing, and a coil of wire. Had Jean Claude left the key in the ignition Greenberg might have climbed in the front and driven off. Jean Claude was keeping his back to them. Perhaps he was having a change of heart. Perhaps he was giving Greenberg the opportunity to do something heroic—the key in the ignition too easy, no, this time Greenberg would have to be more daring, more ingenious. He got out. Althusser followed. They stood by the half-collapsed building. Four severed deer legs bound with twine leaned in a corner. The sun was muted, the wind blew, and continents of grey cloud slid in tectonic slabs across the sky.

Greenberg tried thinking of something safe and banal to say, anything to ease the mood. "So," he began. "Kennedy and Khrushchev came to their senses."

Jean Claude did not respond.

Althusser whistled airily.

"Must have been the hot dog," said Greenberg, referring to Khrushchev's state visit three years ago and the footage of him in a Stetson chowing down on a 'dog in Des Moines.

Nothing. Only the far howl of the wind. He longed for hot sun and thought of Mexico. He predicted great things for Mexico, because like China it was a sleeping giant, but closer, less alien. He never did meet Rivera or Kahlo and now they were dead, though there must be a new generation coming into its own that could benefit from his insight and guidance. When this grisly business was done, he should drive down and spend the winter, get a tan, he tanned well.

Jean Claude exhaled with a terrible finality then took a step back so that he was behind Althusser. Greenberg could scarcely keep from whimpering as he watched Jean Claude's hand slide up under his sweater and grip something. At that moment there was the sound of a latch releasing, the groan of stressed metal. They turned. The car trunk was open and a man was climbing out, a naked man, who stood there looking at them. He was about seventy, balding, bearded, a pale sunken chest, drooping belly, desiccated groin, limbs grue-somely lean, knees swollen knobs, and on his feet sagging red socks. Squinting at the three of them in the field by the shed, the man began backing away one slow step at a time, then turned and began running, pathetic buttocks flapping like dugs.

When the man was no bigger than a dog on the road, the three looked at each other and began to laugh. It was as if the props had been pulled from the stage and it was time to drop their roles and leave the theatre. A mood of innocence took hold. Unburdened, they stood with their hands in their pock-ets and shoulders relaxed; Greenberg thought perhaps they could all travel together to Mexico. Louis could visit the site where Trotsky had been assassinated.

"This is a strange land," said Jean Claude."

"I will not talk, Jean Claude. I will not..." said Althusser, and added in his best American accent, "spill the beans. I am no stoolie."

"Louis." There was a quiet pleading in Jean Claude's tone, a call for dignity.

"The French government is killing itself. It does not need my help. It is driving the stake into its own heart. It has nothing to fear from me."

"I have a duty."

"It was your duty that—" But Althusser did not finish his remark.

"Come." Jean Claude led them back to the car. They all went to the trunk and looked in. There was a blanket and an empty whisky bottle. Jean Claude pressed the trunk lid shut.

"I can vanish," said Althusser, as if it was a party trick that he had mastered.

"They want proof."

"My head?"

"A finger."

"Take one. I have ten." He held his hands out.

"They won't let you live," said Jean Claude. "If it is not me, it will be someone else, someone cruel."

"Ah, so you are kind."

Jean Claude would not be taunted. "Come." They took their places in the car and Jean Claude pulled out onto the road and drove.

"They let Sartre live. He never shuts up. *Bapbapbapbap*. Like a woodpecker."

"It is not my decision."

"But you carry it out."

Jean Claude gripped the steering wheel tightly.

"You carry it out," repeated Althusser, more to himself than Jean Claude. "It is a strange phrase. Like the trash. You carry it out. I am the trash of the state. I have begun to stink. I will corrupt the body politic if I am allowed to linger." He picked up the clown Madeleine had given him and talked to it. "Is that not so my friend."

The clown grinned.

"Sartre did not strangle his wife," said Jean Claude through clenched teeth.

"You blame me for your wife's death."

"Do not speak of her."

"So I am to be silenced. I am a dangerous voice. A threat to the government." There was pride in his tone. "You see, my friend," he said to the clown, "I am formidable."

"Louis," said Jean Claude at last, "the government does not care. It is content for you to go to the hospital. It is the son."

Althusser stared at Jean Claude. Greenberg observed Althusser's profile, the bird-like nose, sharp chin, and a frown, first of scorn and then of confusion. "Son? This is nonsense. I have no son."

"But Hélène did. And this boy, he blames you."

"Hélène? A son?" He threw the clown onto the seat. "No. Never."

"It is true. She was a teenager. Fifteen, sixteen. In Poland."

"Impossible. She had no secrets."

"Louis."

Althusser fell silent. Even the Packard seemed to run more quietly. "So he came to you."

"Yes.

"With money."

"Yes."

"To kill the man who murdered his mother."

Jean Claude said nothing.

"And what about Greenbairg? He is a witness." Althusser turned to look at Greenberg. "Ah. You have made an accord. Did you *shake on it*?" he asked, once again dropping into his gangster voice. "Did you *spit on your hand* first? No? But then the contract is null and void. It has not glue."

"It will be fast."

"I was looking forward to my electric shock," said Althusser, half wry, half sincere. "Have I told you about electric shock?"

"You told us."

"And my LSD. I was hoping to meet God. Instead, I will meet the Devil."

"We should have a last drink." Greenberg held up the bottle that Madeleine had given him.

Relief leapt in Jean Claude's eyes. "Yes. Good."

Greenberg pulled the cork and passed the bottle forward and Jean Claude swigged then passed the bottle to Althusser who seemed dubious. He tilted it warily toward his nose and then sipped.

"Go on, Louis," said Jean Claude. "A big one."

"It will be easier for me, is that it?"

"For you, for me, for all of us."

Althusser sipped again, then passed the bottle to Greenberg. The liquor ran like lava down his throat. Pollock, now there was a man who could pound it back, but in this if in nothing else Greenberg could match him. Plus when Pollock got hosed he was always having to pee. A weak bladder that boy. Greenberg had been there the time he walked in blind drunk and stark naked and pissed in the fireplace. No one knew whether to be appalled or impressed. And the stench! All that asparagus. Greenberg gauged the level of booze that remained, a quarter bottle. Jean Claude pulled over by a dirt road that ran perpendicular to the one they were on, shut off the ignition and once again they sat listening to the motor tick and the wind blow.

"Did he ever get back?" asked Greenberg.

"Who?"

"The King of Dahomey."

"No. In fact he did not. He died. His dogs howled so long and so loud that people came to look and they found them sitting on his chest. Another day and they would have begun to eat him." There was a grim vindication in Althusser's tone, as if betrayal lurked within even the closest relationships.

Greenberg tried to think of something else to say, some means of delaying the inevitable. His hands, seeking places to hide, slipped into his coat pockets and found the five Tuinals. He slid them like magic beans into the whisky bottle.

☙❧

Check-in was straightforward. Patients often arrived sedated or unconscious so there was no alarm, and a wheelchair at hand. A room with a view over a grassy expanse of shrubs was waiting. They provided Althusser's passport and filled out forms, talked with the resident psychologist and head nurse. Greenberg, who hated hospitals almost as much as he hated Rosenberg, had to admit that the place was actually rather reassuring, especially after the chaos of the past week. If they had offered him a bed he might well have said yes. They shook hands with the psychiatrist, a man named Samuel O. Shepchi, and the nurse, a formidable woman named Mrs. Cathcart, and then stepped outside. It was early Monday evening though already impressively dark. A few more hours and they could be in Emma Lake, but it had been a traumatic week capped off with a near catastrophic afternoon, best to

GRANT BUDAY / 139

get a room and arrive fresh the next day in a calmer frame of mind. With one last look at the cupola topping the hospital's main building, they walked beneath the leafless trees to the old Packard.

Standing by the car Greenberg asked, not for the first time, "Have we gone too far?"

Althusser looked at him with great sobriety. "Perhaps not far enough."

"Let's find a hotel."

"The Fish and Fowl," said Althusser. "I am expected."

Greenberg was confused.

"Do not worry, my friend," Althusser assured him, "it is under control." He held his hand out for the key. "I will drive."

The Tuinal-dosed liquor had taken only minutes. By the time they'd walked down the dirt road to the coulee intended to be Althusser's grave, Jean Claude's legs were rubber. Greenberg had to catch his elbow to keep him from stumbling down the slope. Jean Claude began to mutter in French, and then he wheeled and staggered, eyes wide with alarm and accusation. With a desperate effort, Jean Claude had lunged but his knees gave out and Greenberg lowered him to a sitting position, legs splayed out like an infant. Jean Claude's last words were: "I will get you, Greenbuh..."

"He's going to come after me," said Greenberg.

"You will be long gone," Louis assured him.

"I'd better be." Greenberg gazed into the twilight at the uncertainty of his future. Perhaps he'd be going to Mexico after all.

At the wheel of the Packard, Althusser said, "He is a proud man."

"Yes."

"A patriot."

"Dangerous men, patriots," observed Greenberg as if he'd known all too many. "I dare say Swen's a patriot, too."

They recalled Swen in silence.

After awhile, Louis said, "I cannot believe she never told me she had a son." His voice came forlorn from the car's dim interior.

"The war," said Greenberg.

"Yes," said Louis, "*La guerre*."

"Would you have adopted him?"

Louis opened his mouth to speak then stopped.

Greenberg had trouble imagining Louis Althusser as a father figure, still, he tried thinking of something to say, some words of solace, but what came to mind was David's sixteenth birthday. Greenberg had taken the train down to Philadelphia and then got a cab to the house. Not quite a colonial mansion, but damn near. Her niblets had rebounded well from their divorce. The WASP network had forgiven her lapse in having married a Jew. Greenberg liked to think that his reputation even added a measure of notorious cachet. The living room was a swarm of suits and gowns. He'd grabbed a Scotch—she could always be counted on for some decent single malt—shook Robertson's long, pale hand, remarked upon the Grant Wood, and found his way up a set of wide, shallow oak stairs and along a corridor to David's room. His son was lying on his bed reading a *Sgt. Rock* comic book. A scrum of soldiers and word balloons: *Whap! Bam! Krauts!* Greenberg sat on the end of the bed. David was wearing a suit; the polish of his shoes smelled faintly toxic. The walls were covered in movie posters, William Holden in *Stalag 17*, William Holden in *Bridge on the River Kwai*, Holden in *The Bridges at Toko-Ri*. The shelves cluttered with models of fighter planes and space ships and a book titled *Aliens Walk Among Us*.

"Why weren't you in the war?" The boy's voice came

through the comic book, which he kept raised like a screen.

"I didn't get drafted."

"You could have volunteered."

An old issue. Greenberg had been here before. "They had plenty of guys."

David turned a page. "Do you know any forgers?"

"You need cash?"

"I wanna quit school and join up. Mom won't sign the papers."

Greenberg considered his son. A couple of years in the army might slap him into shape and give him some direction. Plus it would piss the queen off and bring he and David closer. He could feel David waiting for him to make the offer. There were still some fifty thousand US soldiers in Korea. There were nine hundred "advisers" in Vietnam and plans underway to send more. In two years it would be 1960 and PFC David Greenberg, eighteen years old, might well find himself on a flight to Southeast Asia—and be back a few months later in a wheelchair or body bag. Greenberg stood. "I got you a record player for your birthday." He waited for him to lower the copy of *Sgt. Rock*. "Yoo hoo."

The comic book went down and their gazes met. Greenberg saw his own eyes and mouth and nose, though the boy's hair was blond and complexion pale.

"Stay in school, sport."

"Sure." The comic book went back up. "Maybe we'll dissect a frog or read *Silas Marner*."

A month later, her highness got a call from a recruitment centre saying David had tried enlisting with false documents. Greenberg was proud of the boy's initiative though disappointed in his draughting skills. A year later, David was in a room in Bellevue staring at a white wall.

❦

They found the Fish and Fowl, a small motel with a flashing neon sign of a trout leaping over a duck. The office was lit up as was the adjoining coffee shop, which had fishing and hunting scenes stencilled on the windows.

"There she is!" cried Louis as he pulled into the lot.

He was out of the car hurrying toward the café waving his hand to a woman in one of the booths. Greenberg followed, battling an icy wind. Louis wrestled open the glass door and they tumbled into a warm refuge of muted conversation and quiet cutlery and the steamy smells of soup and steak. The woman was smiling as Louis slid into the booth beside her and took both her hands in his own and kissed them passionately. Dot.

The café had a liquor license and Greenberg drank three double Canadian Clubs while the reunited lovers cooed. One of Louis's hands stayed busy under the table causing Dot to smile with amused indulgence. Greenberg ordered a fourth drink and through the curved lens of liquor watched them with a not quite detached interest. He tried reconstructing, step by step, the course of Althusser's mind. How had he known? What had he known? If Greenberg had let Jean Claude go through with it, how long would Dot have waited here? He imagined days passing and hope fading like winter light from her eyes. But mad, sly, scrawny, suspicious Althusser had come through, just as he had come through the war and the murder.

The beds in the Fish and Fowl were not of the best quality. The mattress felt like a rubber raft with a leak, the wallpaper was printed with images of men in hip-waders fishing in streams or firing shotguns at ducks. The room had no TV and no minibar, only a black plastic radio the size of a toaster. He dialled through the static, heard a smear of French and then some Slavic language, and finally a snatch of English: "crisis averted...Castro embittered...the Roughriders in third place in the Western Conference with eight wins, seven losses, and one tie..." He opened the drawer of the side table and picked up the Bible, weighed it, considered reading a few chapters, then tossed it back in and shut the drawer with a thump.

He got out of bed and parted the blinds and saw snowflakes tumbling through the light of a street lamp and blanching the ground.

He thought of Emma Lake and the young artists awaiting his direction, and he thought of Rosenberg who was enjoying a stellar year, having given talks at Columbia, the Baltimore Museum of Art, MoMA, Brandeis, Oberlin, Cornell, and even a couple of places out in California, and he was topping it all off with Emma Lake. It was so absurd and cruel and baffling that he could almost laugh.

He switched off the lights and stood in the dark. Louis and Dot had taken a room across the corridor and two doors down; nonetheless he could hear their laughter, her shrieks of mock panic, his shouts of carnivorous pursuit. Lighting a cigarette, Greenberg lay on his back on the bed, feeling envious, feeling bemused, feeling relief, and feeling lonely. The iron radiator trembled and ticked while every few minutes the wind gathered itself to rush at the window as if trying to break in. With the glowing end of his Camel, he wrote his name in the air. He drew a star. He drew a valentine with his initials and Helen's. He stubbed the cigarette out in the ashtray on his chest, right atop his heart.

෴

Clement. Let me ask you—
Yes, I loved her.

Did you, Clement?

Why are you always saying my name? What's up with that? Is that Freud or the other guy?

Does it bother you?

It's weird. Say it less and I'll pay you more.

Clemency. Kindness. Pity. These are good things.

Let me tell you about good things. Helen and I were good. The Golden Couple. Us.

Appearances, Clement.

Content follows form.

And did she love you?

...It was coming.

Is that what she said? Tell me what she said.

She laughed.

Laughed? What do you mean she laughed? How did she laugh?

Opened her mouth, ha ha ha.

There is laughter and there is laughter.

Fond. Kind. Sad. I don't know. We drank a lot. She laughed and said love was coming like a sunrise.

And what follows sunrise?

I don't know.

But you do. Sunset. Sunset follows sunrise.

You mean forget her? I'd need a lobotomy.

Not forget. Look ahead. Move on. Stars follow the sunset. And the moon.

Tuesday, 30 October, 1962

They met for breakfast. Louis popping bits of honeyed toast into Dot's mouth and she sweetening his coffee. Later, they stood in the parking lot by Dot's vw. As they shook hands,

Louis pulled Greenberg close and said, "You are a pea in a whistle, my friend, rattling in the wind."

Greenberg wasn't sure what to make of that—that he was a victim, that he was shrill? "Where will you go now?"

The two responded simultaneously, as if it should have been obvious. "Mexico."

They got into the kraut can and backed out and turned, leaving tracks in the snow. Greenberg went to the Packard and sat behind the wheel. Then he got out and went to the trunk and heaved it open. No one.

⚛

On the drive north, the wind hurled itself against the car forcing him to wrestle the wheel to stay on the road. In the fields the snow had been blown into low drifts. The words buffalo and tundra and muskeg came to mind. Eskimo. Hypothermia. Polar bear and seal blubber and the doomed Franklin Expedition. Greenberg had no use for cold. The sole purpose for ice was to be in his Scotch. Once again he wondered why anyone would live here? Why choose Canada when you could come to America? It made no sense.

He reached Saskatoon at four in the afternoon and already it was getting dark. He'd entered a world of black and grey, dirt and stone, flat land and lowering sky. He found a pub and went in and drank tap beer at a terry cloth-covered table amid prairie people. He studied them as though they were a rare species and saw wind-gritted faces, brick-square wrists, eyes and minds attuned to an altogether earthier frequency. The men wore check wool coats and toques or felted jean jackets and Stetsons. They drank from slender almost elegant glasses that looked absurd in their mitt-like hands. On the walls were oils of silos and tractors and hay bales. He thought of Bosch's *Haywain Triptych*, that grim carnival of perversion and punishment, purity and delusion; it was all there, the high and the low, the body and the soul, hope and lapse. He recalled an afternoon spent standing before the original in Madrid. Old Hieronymus was among the top three artists he'd most like to have met, right next to da Vinci who might well be insufferable, and Durer who once rode two weeks to Holland to see the corpse of a whale on a beach.

He settled back in his wooden chair in the pub and closed his eyes. The Cuban Missile Crisis was over, they'd sailed to the abyss, then the ships of state had corrected course, captains saluting, only Castro left ranting on his rock. And Jean Claude, there was also Jean Claude. He opened his eyes.

The pub ceiling was low and the mood subdued with the onset of winter. He envisioned furred barbarians descending from out of the north and laying siege for the next half year. When he emerged it was six o'clock and black but there were stars and the thin crust of snow glittered as it crunched under the soft heels of his Hush Puppies.

◦◦◦

The first thing he saw when he reached Emma Lake that night was a banner announcing that Art Is In The Making, painted in bold, black letters a yard high. The banner hung between trees and was outlined in blinking green and gold Christmas lights. It looked like a display at a carnival and Greenberg had no doubt who the barker would be. He looked around for an office, some place to find the room—the suite—he'd been promised. He followed voices that rang clear in the cold, dry air. The path was frozen dirt, its ridges pressing through the soles of his thin shoes. Why hadn't they warned him how frigid it would be? Why wasn't there anyone here to greet him? On either side stood rows of cabins, to be honest pretty sorry looking accommodation. Turning up his collar he hunched his shoulders and spotted some sort of auditorium; he approached with dread.

As soon as he stepped inside an officious young woman in a tight black roll-neck sweater and a ponytail issued him safety goggles, a shower cap, and a set of overalls made of heavy-grade waxed paper. Fear seared his insides. Were they expecting radioactive fall-out? Had the news been wrong, had the unholy trinity of Kennedy, Khrushchev, and Castro gone and launched the missiles after all? Was the White House a heap of smoking rubble, was a mushroom cloud hovering over the remains of New York, the Hudson River on fire, people leaping from the upper floors of the Empire State Building? He looked to the young woman with her smooth skin and severe glasses, her whole life...

"Hurry up and get dressed," she said, giving him a shove. "The show's starting."

An elderly couple were trying to insert themselves into their outfits. Greenberg joined them and all three hopped and staggered about the foyer. How insulting that neither the young woman nor the elderly couple recognized him.

When they entered the gallery proper it was as though they were joining a lab experiment, or a themed sex party where everyone wore baby sleepers. In the middle of the gallery was a roped-off rectangle, one end of which was a wall, and in this enclosure stood a young man about twenty-five, naked, his hairless body like something from a weightlifting magazine. The women in the crowd were still and watchful; the men sucked in their bellies and squared their shoulders. Greenberg had partaken in a few Manhattan evenings involving inflatable girls, mescal, baby pythons, but this was wholly unexpected in Saskabush.

Rosenberg glided through the crowd with his head high—how the bastard loved being tall—lower lip bulbous beneath a moustache that made Greenberg think of a muskrat pelt. Their eyes met. Rosenberg grinned and called out, "Boyo! Beginning to think they nabbed you at the border!"

People frowned. They leaned and whispered, *Surely that wasn't Greenberg...*

By way of acknowledgment, Greenberg elevated an eyebrow, curled one corner of his mouth, raised his chin and nodded once.

The bare-ass guy was mucking about with a table full of paint. He had squirt guns, grease guns, sponges, a trowel, a soup ladle, a roller, and a dozen brushes more suited to painting the hull of a ship than a canvas. Rosenberg stork-stepped over the gold silk cord and put his arm around the artist and gave him a manly squeeze then a resounding thwack across the chest with an open palm. In his other hand he held a microphone like a pro, a veritable Bobby Darrin, executing neat moves with the mic wire.

"Lay-dees and gennelmen!" He launched into some hoo-ha about how pleased he was to see so many here for an event the likes of which, "I am pretty damn sure will mark a serious break from the rut of tradition. But as they say, action speaks and words, well, words are talk. So without further ado put your safety glasses on and make sure your seat belts are fastened." He gave Greenberg another wink, faked a left hook to the kid's gut, and said, "Go to it, champ." Scissor-stepping back over the rope he nodded to a sixtyish woman Greenberg recognized as Angela van Dieman, editor of the journal *Blue Kangaroo*, a woman who had repeatedly rebuffed Greenberg and touted Rosenberg, a woman who'd been Frieda Kahlo's lover, Brecht's lover, Picasso's plaything, a guest of Dali, had drunk with Beckett, and caused a Venetian cardinal to hurl himself into the Grand Canal. She offered Greenberg a nod; she may not like him, but she could not ignore him. Greenberg responded in kind, then crossed his arms over his chest and faced the artist waiting to be impressed.

The kid went in hard. Dunked a brush as wide as his hand into a gallon can of red and did not merely fling paint but threw the whole brush. It hit the wall and snakes of colour flew everywhere. The brush bounced with a sloppy clatter.

Rosenberg said, "With that first shot alone the artist has broken with the convention of picture-on-wall, for it now includes the floor as well as the brush itself, an artifact of the art-making process."

This was met with whispers of approval. Notes were made. Greenberg studied the expressions around him and saw a willing suspension of disbelief: the schmucks were buying it.

The kid followed with not one but two brushes, hurling them simultaneously. He plunged his hands directly into the cans and windmilled gobs of paint. This led to taking up the cans themselves and flinging the contents. Then he pitched the cans as well. They clattered and oozed and soon the ceiling became assimilated in the art event along with the floor. The kid shouted as he worked, erupting in Tourette's-like streams of swearing so sexist, racist, and blasphemous that some of the more elderly fled the gallery in horror.

More left when the kid went up to the wall and rubbed his butt against it.

"Be strong, people, be strong," urged Rosenberg, sensing the strain.

Cameras were flashing. People scribbled in notebooks. Two men with movie cameras ducked and weaved.

The kid now advanced upon the wall in a slinky strut all pelvis and thigh and began to hump the wet paint, his buttocks flexing. Angela van Dieman moved closer. The boy put his fists on his hips and began peeing on the wall, the urine steaming. Done, he turned and strolled back to the table and for his next move poured a bucket of black paint followed by one of yellow down his chest and, screaming, ran at the wall with such mad-bull abandon that he bounced and lay stunned. The sound had been sickening. A fist on flesh, a body dropped on brick. The crowd winced. Many turned away. One woman vomited.

Rosenberg continued his exegesis. "This is the arena of struggle, my friends, this is it. Conflagration. Conflict. War. Behold fallen Icarus after his mad rush at the sun, see Diony-sus flung from the horse, the *uber* artist burned in the fire of the synthesis of ego and id."

The two filmmakers leaned over the rope for close-ups. The kid was bleeding from the ears. Lying on his back, breathing hoarsely, his arms and legs groped and twitched in the muddy slough of colour. He also had an erection. Angela van Die-man tore at her paper suit, stripped off her black blouse and canary yellow pants, crawled on hands and knees under the gold rope and lay herself naked alongside the fallen warrior with her cheek to his chest and her arms encircling his head. The flashbulbs poofed and their lights gleamed in the paint like phosphorescence in a midnight sea.

After a suitable interlude during which Angela alternately wept then moaned, she was encouraged to allow a veterinar-ian in the audience to examine the young artist. The man's expertise was in de-worming cattle, but he performed a thor-ough examination and declared that the lad was a tough young buck. A blanket was folded to form a stretcher and the hero was carried out like a Spartan on his shield.

Chairs were unfolded and a discussion ensued, Rosenberg presiding. "As we have experienced all too recently, Armaged-don looms. The Cold War entombs us in its icy mausoleum. There is no competing with the radiance of the sun!" He paused to let this *aperçu* sink in. "Art should *lead*, not trail science. It must regain its pre-eminence. Orgasm!" He nodded solemnly letting them know that they had indeed heard correctly. "We want nothing less than an explosion. Not a mindless burst but a physical fulfilment." Beating time on his palm he stated, "We must break the bonds that hobble the creative spirit, and that means plunging into the volcano."

Seated at the rear of the room, Greenberg watched the people nod and murmur their approval. Eager to demonstrate their grasp of the concept, a few confessed that they would never be content with the conventions of the gallery experience again. "You've ruined me," said one woman ecstatically.

Rosenberg responded with a smile and sized her up and down for a midnight rendezvous.

"Art is now a form of dance," he decreed, arms flung wide, "one in which artist and audience participate equally. Think of Shiva. Envision a ballet of fire in which we all combust."

Greenberg yawned loudly. He would not be such a prosaic schlub as to ask where all this left the gallery and the collector, much less the artist—other than the burn ward.

Tea and cookies were served.

Wednesday, 31 October, 1962

Whenever he couldn't sleep, Greenberg recited the ever-lengthening list of insults he'd endured. His father called him lazy and ungrateful, his brother Martin said he was selfish and a bully, his therapist said he was self-obsessed and emotionally stunted while Mary McCarthy—the bitch who he might have loved—said he was sadistic, odious, and overbearing. Kozloff said he oversimplified the complex, Dubois said he made things needlessly complicated, Sylvia Sabatini said he was a drunk and a lousy lover, Irene Katz said he was a self-hating Jew and a homosexual in denial, Beth Majors said his writing was vague and tentative, Derwent Finnegan said that he wrote with a fence post, and Rosenberg said his views were haphazard and sophomoric, and that he was an arrogant pedant who spewed absolute value judgments with the finesse of a gatling gun. This was only to list the highlights.

Shooting Rosenberg would be efficient but too quick. He wanted to draw it out, get a knife, a big knife, preferably one with a serrated blade, one used for skinning and gutting, then start in on a finger, then a toe, move on to an ear, maybe stab him once in each butt cheek.

Rosenberg had the cabin across the path. There'd been shrieks and laughter earlier; now there was snoring. Lacking either a gun or a knife he supposed he could sneak on over and smother the bastard and then claim insanity like Althusser. He'd been in therapy going on six years, surely that had to stand in his favour even if nobody in the art community would go to bat for him.

But he stayed where he was. The mattress felt as if it had been filled with gravel. He rolled onto his side and heard his heartbeat. He hated hearing his heartbeat, it reduced him to a pump and tubes. Was that what it all came down to, hydraulics? He turned onto his other side. There hadn't been a drop of liquor at the event this evening. He rolled onto his stomach; the mattress smelled funny. He rolled onto his back once more and felt exposed. He began to appreciate Althusser's eagerness for electroshock.

It was dawn before he was mercifully freed from consciousness and fell asleep and midmorning when he woke from a dream of playing catch with David. At first he tossed the ball underhand, but David, all of seven, thought that was for babies, overhand, it had to be overhand, like in the big leagues, so Greenberg threw him a few overhand, not hard but with a bit of stink on them, and David caught them in his new glove. Then he misjudged and the ball bonked him on the forehead. David dropped onto his rear, stunned, frowning, not sure whether he was hurt or had somehow been betrayed. Getting up he threw down the glove and marched into the house leaving Greenberg standing there feeling guilty and confused because he hadn't known what to do, how to react, jolly him out of it or rush up all concerned?

He dressed in the same lank and grubby clothes he'd been wearing all week. His lower back was rigid, his neck tight, and his eye still ached though it functioned. Stepping outside he found Rosenberg smoking in the sun.

"Clem, buddy."

"Harry."

They didn't shake hands.

Rosenberg smoked fiercely, holding the cigarette like a dart and squinting in judgement of the day. "Looks like you took one," he said, indicating Greenberg's eye.

Rosenberg was looking like the lord of the manor in a black-and-tan checked tweed coat and matching scarf. Greenberg was freezing in his sport jacket and khakis.

"Canada," said Rosenberg. *Kee-a-nuh-duh*.

"I hear there are polar bears," said Greenberg.

"Let's walk."

The path ran through stunted trees.

"Saw Oldenburg in the city last week, guy's talking about doing giant clothespins. I said that's swell, Claes. How about some giant moo cows while you're at it?" He shook his head.

"Quite the show last night," said Greenberg.

"Hope the ambulance didn't disturb you," said Rosenberg. "The horse doc had second thoughts and figured the kid had gone and concussed himself. Angela went with him. I think the old bird's in heat."

"Got another one of those?"

Rosenberg passed him a Pall Mall and his lighter. Greenberg savoured the brief sweet scent of lighter fluid and then the soothing burn of the smoke deep in his chest. The path skirted the lake. Could Rosenberg swim? They paused at a small dock. The water was shallow, the bottom gravel and sand, the bean pole would just stand up demanding what the fuck! He'd have to knock him unconscious. A rock, he needed a rock, but there were people about and they seemed keenly aware of Greenberg and Rosenberg... *and then Mr. Greenberg he, I don't know, he just picked up a rock, a pretty big rock, and well he hit Mr. Rosenberg on the head*... Did they have capital punishment in Canada? Or would he spend the rest of his life in prison with a bunch of Canucks? Unless it was the nuthouse. Electroshock and LSD down there in Weyburn with Jean Claude. He spotted a fist-sized stone and picked it up hefting it in his hand and marvelling at its weight. Was Canadian stone heavier? Did it have to do with being so far north? He gripped the stone until his fingers hurt and his nails went white and thought of those guys in the Olympics in Greece doing the shot put. Now there was an event with pedigree. Putting the shot, hurling the discus, and wrestling, that Greco-Roman business, naked. Did Greco-Roman women wrestle naked? Dropping the stone into the lake it made a *basso profundo kerplunk*.

"You look beat, Clem."

He wiped grit from his palm and shrugged his shoulders against the chill. "Where the hell are we?"

Rosenberg cackled and passed him another butt. They smoked and looked at the lake. Grey-blue water abraded here and there by wind, while elsewhere polished as a mirror.

Rosenberg yawned. "So you got a little lecture all prepped for us?" He yawned again. "Not the old trinity, I hope. Cézanne, Braque, Pollock. Between you and me, you really oughta junk that and chart a new course. You've fallen into a rut. Gnawed that one to the bone."

A public space devoted to stoning blasphemers. That's what they needed. Every person in the polis hurling rocks down on the offender's head, pounding him to his knees, reducing him to a bloody lump for the vultures. Greenberg gazed up and was pleased to see a couple of eagles spiralling above the lake.

"I need a coffee," said Greenberg.

"I need a drink," said Rosenberg. He cocked an eyebrow. "You game?"

"Is the pope a Yid?"

They hoofed it back to his cabin.

Rosenberg definitely had the superior room. Bigger, brighter, the bed newer, the rugs cleaner, the chair in the corner firm and plush without even a strip of duct tape on it; the place even smelled better. Rosenberg decanted a generous splash of Laphroaig into a sturdy Scotch glass. On the bureau sat an open case lined with red velvet moulded to hold two glasses and a bottle. Give him credit, he treated himself right. Greenberg decided that he had to have one for himself, maybe that one. "Cheers." Rosenberg winked.

Greenberg drank and nearly wept in relief at the taste of a good peaty Scotch instead of the carpet cleaner he'd been swilling.

"Let us now praise the Scots for their two great contributions to culture," said Rosenberg. "Laphroaig and Robert Louis Stevenson."

Greenberg was almost inclined to wonder if he'd misjudged the son of a bitch. Rosenberg reclined on the bed with his ankles crossed and his drink balanced on his chest while Greenberg took the chair in the corner and groaned as if sinking into a hot bath.

"So, two days late. Met a little someone en route, did you?"

"Bit of a bumpy trip. You know Althusser?"

"Frog that throttled his wife?"

He was ready to tell the tale but first needed a top-up. He made a show of bewilderment at the state of his near empty glass.

"Bar's open. Help yourself."

Greenberg tilted the bottle, pleased to note that it was three-quarters full—was there any more reassuring sight?—and filled his glass halfway to the brim. Booze. Maybe it was that simple. Forget art and philosophy and love, it all came down to Scotch. He sipped and joy pulsed like a revelation. He refilled Rosenberg's glass and they rolled the fuming liquor around their mouths. Smoke and moss and honey and a hint of the bee's sting. It was already hitting him where it counted, delivering a sweet corrosion in his empty belly. Yes, it had been a helluva trip and would make a damn fine book. He was long overdue to try his hand at a novel. Or would it be a memoir? Glass to his lips he breathed the heady vapour. Call it *Atomic Road*.

"That was some crazy crap you peddled last night, Harry."

Rosenberg said nothing.

Greenberg waited. "I mean come on."

Rosenberg slowly swirled his glass and frowned with those hedge-like eyebrows.

"That kid, what was he, some farm boy?"

Rosenberg frowned and studied the wall.

"Or you spring him from the nuthouse down the road?"

Rosenberg drew in a long breath and eased it back out.

What's this? Greenberg's glass was empty again. That wouldn't do at all. He resisted the urge to lick it. Rosenberg still had a couple of fingers worth in his. What an amateur. Fine. Greenberg bided his time. The Scotch was rolling in like a high tide while the light was taking on the amber glow of those California kelp beds. What year had that been? '34?

'36? He'd spent a whole month swimming and lying around in Big Sur. He decided he'd go back there and write the book. But what he needed right now was another wee snort. He heaved himself forward and snagged the bottle by the neck and glugged some into his glass and sat back admiring the tint, the same as that sun-shot Big Sur seawater. He sipped and held it in his mouth until his teeth felt like they were dissolving and his tongue prickled and his brain basked and only then did he swallow. It hit his gut like a depth charge. He rode out the wave that spread through his belly all the way to his hands and head and feet and then he stood. Heaved himself upright. How tall he felt. A *mensch*. He was disappointed in JFK for not bombing Cuba to the bottom of the sea, flattening the Urals, reducing Siberia to slag and wiping Moscow off the map. How festive the afterglow would have been. And when the embers settled into a somber radiance it would usher in an era of quiet dignity not seen since the Athens of Pericles. And yet what had happened? Nothing. Detente. Sweet zip-all. What kind of men were they? Worse, here was Rosenberg laid out nice and smug on the bed in shiny new brogues and with an expression on his mug that said he was King Kong. Well, that just wouldn't do at all. Greenberg stood, unzipped his trousers, tugged out his schlong and pissed on him.

Rosenberg howled. Leapt as if jabbed with a cattle prod. Greenberg roared and ran at him. Butted him in the belly with his head driving him into the wall. Rosenberg locked his arms around Greenberg's neck and kneed him in the chest. They fell. Greenberg gulped for breath aware of Rosenberg doing the same. He was also acutely aware that his zipper was still down. He tugged it up and in one motion rolled toward Rosenberg and swung his fist but Rosenberg also did a roll and Greenberg's fist struck the wood floor. Pain shot up his knuckles through his wrist to his elbow. Rosenberg now punched Greenberg on the forehead. A white flower bloomed in time-lapse speed behind Greenberg's eyes. Rosenberg got to his knees and Greenberg had just enough savvy to wriggle away. He found himself under the bed. With a shout, Rosenberg did a swan dive onto it. The mattress, supported by a mesh of metal strapping, crushed Greenberg for an instant then sprang back. Rosenberg jumped up and did it again. Before he could do it a third time, Greenberg rolled out the other side, stood, and hurled himself onto Rosenberg's back on the bed and put the sleeper on him. As a boy he'd watched the professional wrestlers in Madison Square Garden. Red Devil Robinson, The Grim Reaper, Johnny Cain, and everyone's favourite Mr. Syd, who had only one arm and always lost but put up a heroic battle. Rosenberg's long arms flailed and slapped. He pushed himself up to his hands and knees and rolled over so that Greenberg was underneath him. But Greenberg held on. Kept that sleeper going. They strained and made gurgling noises. Rosenberg bit Greenberg's wrist. Greenberg shouted and they both rolled and fell off the bed. Riding Rosenberg to the floor Greenberg got his hands around his throat. None of your sleepers or half nelsons now, they were past that, just straightforward strangulation. Greenberg cursed inarticulately while Rosenberg gurgled like a stuck pig. He peeled Greenberg's fingers from his neck and bent them back until Greenberg yelped. They squared off once again, this time in wrestling crouches, circling each other crabwise, arms up like pincers. Rosenberg threw a jab. Greenberg saw it coming. He registered it clearly in his mind: a fist, growing bigger and bigger—but forgot to move, too diverted by the recollection that the perception of size was directly related to the amount of light reaching the eye. Luckily, Rosenberg's accuracy was bad and the punch only grazed Greenberg's ear. He tackled Rosenberg about the hips slamming him into the wall dislodging a heavy-framed print that thumped Rosenberg on the top of the head. Rosenberg collapsed and the print lay upside down against the wall. Modigliani: *Bride and Groom.*

Chest heaving, Greenberg stood over him. "Get up, you bastard!" He shouted this even though he wanted him to stay down, for the fight to be done, for Rosenberg to be so thoroughly drubbed that the next time they met he would flinch with fear. "Come on. Up!"

Rosenberg didn't move.

Greenberg wiped his sweaty forehead with the back of his wrist. "Hey."

Rosenberg didn't respond.

Greenberg nudged him with his foot.

Nothing.

Realization burned through the fog of booze: he'd killed him—in hand-to-hand combat. Holy shit... Self-defence! It had been self-defence... He looked around. Call the cops? Stuff him into bed and pull up the covers and sneak out? He checked the washroom—no window. He tottered back into the room and put his ear to the door. Could he slip out unseen, play innocent?

"Rosenberg...Harry..."

His mouth was open and his tongue lolling.

Scotch swirling through his skull, he clapped his hands to his head and turned in a circle and moaned. People must have heard them fighting. He was a mess, his hand was swollen, and he'd never hold up under questioning. The room was stifling. He tugged at his collar. He couldn't breathe. Swinging the door open he reeled out the door shouting, "I've killed him, I've killed Rosenberg! My God! My God!" He slapped himself about the face, pulled at his fringe of hair. Doors from the other cabins opened and young artists peered out. "I've killed him!" Greenberg covered his eyes with his palms as if to block out the memory, then dropped them and stared with new hope. "Is there a doctor? Where's that veterinarian? Is he still here?" He whirled to rush back in to check Rosenberg's pulse and ran straight into him standing in the doorway.

"You putz. You got in a lucky shot." And slugged Greenberg in the chest knocking him on his arse.

Thursday, 1 November, 1962

The radio report described the acrobatic escape from the Weyburn Mental Hospital. The patient, one Louis Althusser, leapt from a second story window and ran off into the night. The RCMP were on the lookout.

Greenberg had driven all night, planning to strike straight south through Fargo and then angle on down to Chicago and back to New York. He could stay with his brother, or get a hotel, or a new apartment, or even hole up with David, but he knew that eventually Jean Claude would find him, for eventually Greenberg would go to a gallery, to an opening, to an exhibition, give a lecture, after all he had to resume his life or what was the point? He supposed he could contact the police and get Jean Claude arrested—but on what charge? Having been drugged and checked into the Weyburn Psychiatric Hospital under the name of Louis Althusser? How could Jean Claude be blamed for having tried—and succeeded—in escaping? The radio report did not say whether he was armed or dangerous, but Greenberg knew better and feared both.

By the time he reached Winnipeg he had a new plan: he did not head south-east for Chicago but south-west back toward Haaden Creek. Jean Claude would show up there sooner or later. Meanwhile Greenberg would have time to explain and get Madeleine on side. After all, Greenberg and Althusser had done Jean Claude a huge favour by preventing him from becoming a murderer. The Weyburn escapade was just that, a prank, a lark, and if it was a little inconvenient that was unfortunate but it was better than the electric chair, better than not seeing Madeleine again. Surely she'd understand this and talk sense to Jean Claude, temper him. Money, of course, would help. Greenberg would pay the ten thousand as agreed, or perhaps they could compromise at five, either way, money or no, the lovely couple would have each other and live happily ever after in Haaden Creek while Greenberg went home to New York and wrote up his adventures. Yes, that would do.

Relieved, he stopped at a diner and ate with excellent appetite. As he chowed down the blizzard let up and the sun came out. He filled the tank and got the Packard back out on the highway and laughed: Althusser had a new life, Jean Claude would have a new life, and Greenberg had a book to work on. He lit a Camel and was content. Admittedly Emma Lake had been a fiasco, no keynote speech, no stipend, no feature in *Canadian Art*, but it was hardly his fault, the book would make that clear, and in fiction he'd have his way with Rosenberg; people all across the country would weep with laughter. He needed a pseudonym for the son-of-a-bitch, something to keep the lawyers off, but everyone in on the joke. Horace Rose? Harvey Redbutt?

By the time he crossed the border back into North Dakota, the snow had vanished. He continued on down to Grand Forks before striking west for Minot. It was an easy run on an excellent road. In Grand Forks, he'd topped up the tank again and discovered that last night had been Halloween, the girl behind the counter still wearing a witch's hat. She gave him a candy kiss and he popped it into his mouth and sucked the tarry molasses as he drove, recalling trick-or-treating as a boy, him and his brother, pillowcases over their shoulders weighty with loot. He'd loved Halloween. He and Harold Lazarus had gone trick-or-treating together until they were sixteen. When you were hidden by a mask, who knew your age? He remembered taking David out when he was six. He was living with his mother up in New Hampshire at the time and Greenberg had made the trip especially. It had been fun doing him up as a clown, red nose, curly red wig, red lips, a polka-dotted suit and floppy red shoes. And yet the costume couldn't hide the boy's bewilderment. Maybe it was the fireworks, or the crowds, or maybe it was that Greenberg hadn't seen him in months, or all of it, but David didn't enjoy himself; he seemed near tears the entire evening so Greenberg was disappointed, which David sensed, and that of course made it worse. Coulrophobia. Fear of clowns. Greenberg banged the steering wheel and resolved to give him a call as soon as he got back to New York. Did he have a phone? Didn't matter, he'd just drive on up and they'd have a reunion, he and his son, he and his boy. Goddamn right.

He reached Minot in the late afternoon. The sky was a vast grey slab and he was exhausted, the long night of driving having caught up. The lights were already on in cafés revealing solitary coffee drinkers. He thought of Hopper's *Nighthawks*. He could be in Haaden Creek in another hour and a half, but by then it would be dark and locating Madeleine's place would be dicey. He pulled into a Shell station where a sign advertised Super Shell with Platformate. He used the restroom, and as he splashed his face he looked at himself in the mirror and recalled that Shell station where they'd ditched Jean Claude. He'd come full circle, or not quite, but there was form, a sense of frame. His chest hurt where Rosenberg had socked him. Still, he was pretty damn sure the goof would think twice about tangling with him again, though he may well have gone over the line by peeing on him. He cringed at the thought of word getting round though Pollock was probably applauding from the grave. He checked his wallet. Forty-three dollars. If it were summer, he'd just sleep in the car. He went to the cashier, a kid in a skeleton suit sitting on a stool reading a novel. Alongside jugs of motor oil and tins of car wax there were a dozen or more carved pumpkins with candles lending the small shop a cavernous feel. He asked about a cheap motel.

The kid regarded Greenberg a moment. "The Great Plains. It was fumigated last month."

"The Great Plains."

"Or Musty's."

Greenberg waited for him to laugh. He didn't. He lay the novel spread open on the counter. Greenberg disapproved of that, it stressed the spine. One should always use a bookmark. "*On the Road*," he said, reading the title.

The kid looked at him with wary defiance.

Greenberg didn't mention that he'd met Kerouac and that the guy had been drunk, sullen, belligerent, awkward, needy, self-pitying, self-regarding, and self-obsessed. In short, typical. "You thinking of a road trip?"

"South America. Chile."

"Chile?" Greenberg had met Neruda but didn't mention that either.

The kid pulled the skeleton hood back exposing blond hair. "It's coming on summer down there." Then he added, "I want to get as far away from here as possible." Wistful, he looked out the window past the pumpkins and a poster for Super Shell. The candle flames in the pumpkins complicated the glass, in which Greenberg could see their ghostly reflections. He wondered about growing up in a place like 'My Not' North Dakota, Podunk of the Prairies, but then Pound and

Hemingway had been from out this way and apparently it hadn't hurt them. Was this kid an artist in the making? His eyes looked grave beyond their years. Greenberg could see the candle flames reflected in them. He thought of David up there in New England making candles. They'd be about the same age, David maybe a couple of years older. The one hiding, the other ready to run.

"Khrushchev backed down," he said, reassuringly.

"*This time*," said the kid.

"I think we can breathe easy for a while." Good Christ! Was that him talking? No wonder teenagers distrusted adults.

"Until some cowboy hits the button. Maybe I'll learn Quechua. That's the language of the Inca. Folks still speak it down there. In the mountains," he added, in case Greenberg didn't know that Chile had mountains.

"Didn't they have some massive earthquake and tidal wave just last year?" Greenberg regretted saying this even as it was coming out of his mouth. Typical adult raining on the boy's enthusiasms.

A car slid in alongside the pump and the kid drew his skeleton hood over his head and went out to serve the customer. When he returned he rang up the sale.

Greenberg said, "I don't know about a motel called Musty's."

The kid laughed, which improved his face. He had short teeth, dark brown eyes, a strong chin. He pulled his hood back. "The Great Plains is your best bet."

"Thank you. Say, good luck in South America. Sounds like a great idea. Wish I was going." Greenberg reached across and they shook hands. The kid's was cold and smelled of gasoline.

"Darwin was there," said the kid. "In Chile. In Valparaíso."

For a moment they imagined Charles Darwin walking

around the cobbled streets of Valparaíso on legs wobbly from months at sea.

"Well," said Greenberg.

"Okay," said the kid.

Friday, 2 November, 1962

Madeleine did not look particularly pleased, nonetheless she stepped back without a word letting him enter the kitchen. Wanda was at the table, the two metal balls going around and around in her palm like lucky nickels. The stove cast an inviting aura of heat in contrast to Madeleine's decidedly cool demeanour standing by the door, arms crossed, jaw set.

"I did him a favour. He could've got the chair."

"Uh huh."

"It was haywire."

"And now?"

"Now what?"

"Now what the blue blazes are you doing here is now what."

"We have to talk. Jean Claude and I."

"Discuss old times."

"I owe him money."

The Baoding balls continued to ting and the stove crackled. Greenberg was standing between the two women. He looked at Wanda who was watching the balls go around as though they were rare creatures moving of their own volition. "I need to call New York," he said.

"Go on down to the post office."

Greenberg's glance cut to the phone on the wall. Mentioning the Big Apple hadn't even dented her armour. "I need to arrange for the money."

This was no more successful, if anything her face hardened.

He also needed to pee, but was afraid to ask to use the washroom. Edging closer to the stove he put his hands out for the heat. With its curves and brass it was an impressively elaborate old appliance. He experienced a flash of nostalgia for Edwardian flourish, an appreciation for craft and design.

"I don't know what they did to him in there, but he's not the same," said Madeleine. There was anger and pleading in her tone.

"You've talked? Where's he headed? Here? What did he say?"

"Wasn't so much what he said but how he said it."

"Okay, how did he say it? How did he sound?"

"Different."

Greenberg was about to come up with something to the effect that they'd all changed, but Madeleine reached down and took the shotgun from its spot by the door and levelled it at him.

"Move." She indicated the door.

As he stepped past her she fit the barrel to his back and nudged. He left the embracing aura of the stove and entered icy exile. The wood steps were brittle under his heels, the ground frozen. In just days the earth, the grass, the air, even the light had taken on an Arctic cast. The crows—did they have nothing better to do—mocked from the apple trees like an embittered Greek chorus. Greenberg's jacket and pants felt like sheet metal against his skin. He shoved his hands into his armpits and was relieved to reach the barn and escape the wind. He looked hopefully at the hay thinking he might burrow into it, or get a horse blanket and sleep in one of the cars.

"Look, why—" She thrust the barrel into his back. He stumbled then yelped as he nearly fell into a hole.

"Get the ladder."

"Tie me up by the stove. I'll sit on the floor."

"You'll get the ladder."

He saw it lying by the wall.

"Just let me talk to Jean Claude."

"Seems to me you've talked enough to him. You and that other squirrely guy both."

The ladder was crusted with dirt and dung. He looked around the barn with longing. Why couldn't he just sit by the wall? As he lowered the ladder into the hole, he looked at Madeleine. "I found the box for you. Doesn't that count for something?" A pigeon flapped in the rafters. The barn smelled of old grain and cold earth.

"Down."

He faced her. "No."

She lowered shotgun and for a moment Greenberg thought she might actually smile, say something about him finally growing a spine. She did not, she stepped toward him and they stood nose to nose, the gun gripped like an iron bar in her two fists. He could grab it. He could. Surely he was stronger than her. She stared straight into his eyes, calmly, coolly, utterly devoid of self-doubt. Pollock had had that confidence. He felt her warm breath on his face and smelled her scent of soap. There were lines radiating from the corners of her eyes and her jaw was taut. He heard a tinging. Wanda. Standing in the doorway, the balls swirling like mice in her palm.

Madeleine did not turn from Greenberg as she addressed her sister. "How about you go make us some tea, Wanda."

Greenberg's heart felt like a balloon bobbing to the surface. Wanda turned and went out. Greenberg inclined his head and widened his eyes appealing to Madeleine's sense of reason.

"Down."

"No."

She stepped back while simultaneously swinging the shot-gun like a baseball bat. Greenberg caught the stock of the gun across the meat of his forearm and shoulder. Pain bloomed like a bomb. A moment later he was descending the ladder into the grave-hole smell of dark damp earth, arm hot and aching.

ꙮ

Somewhere along the line Greenberg had lost his wristwatch with its radium dial. He reflected upon the phrase *somewhere along the line*. As if the path leading from the past to the present was linear. He feared there was a dot indicating the end of the line, and that here in this black cellar, this grave that smelled of damp earth, he had reached it.

He looked up at the hole in the ceiling. Madeleine stared down at him. She dropped a box of matches and a couple of candles then returned a quarter of an hour later and lowered a bucket at the end of a rope with a hook. In it was a thermos of tea and a packet of saltines. She deftly let the rope go slack freeing the hook from the bucket handle and began hauling the rope back up. Greenberg grabbed the rope as it was rising past his head and held it. The tension eased. The rope, a sturdy length of cord smooth with use, hung neutral. Would a slight tug communicate his remorse over what had happened? He imagined a form of communication evolving, a morse code of rope tugs with which they might expatiate upon their own biographies, childhood traumas, adolescent yearnings, hopes and dreams, tragedies large and small, and in this manner come to know and respect each other. The rope jumped out of his reach and vanished through the hole. Then something fell on him, hit him with a *whump*. Greenberg cringed, arms up shielding his head. A blanket.

Lighting one of the candles he explored and found some cabbage leaves and a potato and a plank with a nail in it. A cellar, squared out corners with the walls and floor pounded flat. Where was he expected to do his business? The bucket was galvanized metal. He gave it a sniff and detected no odour suggesting that it was a toilet. He stood beneath the hole in the ceiling and shouted: Hey!" Nothing. He shouted again: "Madeleine!" He began to pace. The candle, set on the ground, grew tall and still when he was at the far end of the room, but trembled each time he passed, as though his proximity was deeply disturbing.

He looked at things from Jean Claude's point of view. First Greenberg breaks his toe, then he leaves him in a gas station toilet, then he screws up his mission to execute Althusser, and finally he incarcerates him in an insane asylum. Yes, fine, the man had a few gripes, maybe even a strong case for wishing him harm. He began to feel a creeping fear at what they might well have done to him there: straitjacket, lobotomy, electroshock, drugs, all four? Here in the cellar things looked decidedly bleaker than they had while barrelling along in the car in the sun. It would not do to be here when Jean Claude arrived.

He pissed in the bucket, placed it in the far corner with the plank on top then sat against the wall with his knees up. Even with the blanket his back and butt were damp and cold. He went and sat on top of the plank on the bucket. It stank. It was all Rosenberg's fault. And Althusser's. He should've stayed put in Emma Lake and waited for Jean Claude and dealt with it then and there, or followed Dot and Althusser to Mexico, or headed for Big Sur. He let his head fall forward into his hands, elbows propped on his knees. Last year he'd been at his peak. *Art and Culture* had got rave reviews, Kroll said he was unmatched, Kramer said he had the finest mind of our time, the best since Ruskin, John O'Brian—that young visionary—said he was the most influential critic of the twentieth century, and now here he was in a hole in North Da-fucking-kota awaiting his executioner.

Regrets descended upon him like a rain of dead leaves. His pal Harold Lazarus once said, "Greeny, you're a sophist at heart." Where had they been? The Cape? Atlantic City? He recalled the brine of low tide sand. How confusing that Harold Lazarus—the one man he'd loved—should have the same name as Harold Rosenberg, the one he hated. What symbolism. A bit weighty, a bit obvious, the critics would roll their eyes if he used it in a book, but life was life and art was art, and while the two were entwined they were ever at odds. The fact was he'd always been too self-doubting to be an artist, for all his bluster and balls, for all his scope and insight he was always looking over his shoulder as he wrote, always worrying, always writing his own reviews before he'd even got a first draft down. Maybe he should have enlisted. Look at Mailer. All those guys. War had made them.

In the dark times
Will there also be singing?
Yes, there will be singing
About the dark times.

Brecht. A survivor. He'd seen the smoke, smelled the cordite, heard the cannon, and known when and how to escape, just like Althusser. Greenberg wondered how he himself would have coped over there, wearing a uniform, lugging a pack and a gun, helmet on his head, some square-jawed goombah with a brick for a brain giving him orders, telling him when to jump and where to shit. Would David respect him more if he'd have gone over, and Helen? What was she going to think when she heard about this? *I told him. I called him. I warned him, but he never listened, that was the thing, he never listened, that's why I left, why I had to leave…*

He began scraping toe and finger-holds into the clay wall.

He scraped until his nails were raw then began using the metal lip of the thermos to dig hand-holds as high as he could reach, then emptied the bucket and turned it over and stood on it and dug another notch higher still. He climbed then scraped another hole—left forearm and shoulder weak and sore where she'd walloped him—but the toe-hold gave way and he slid. He tried again with the same result. It was no use, the clay couldn't bear his weight. He was too fat. Bald and fat. He remained on the floor and pulled the blanket over him and stared at the candle flame that was now taller than the nub of wax that supported it, and thought of David pouring wax in his shack in the woods.

David met Helen one time. He was out of Bellevue, pale, overweight, shaky, but decently dressed and clean shaven. It was in Atlantic City, on the boardwalk eating ice cream with his mother. Greenberg and Helen were there for a weekend, the last the two of them ever spent together. When they ran into David and her nibs the conversation had been stilted. So! Wow! Great! Absolutely! Standing there impeding foot traffic, ice cream on David's chin, Greenberg acutely aware of Helen taking in every detail, judging even if she claimed not to. Late summer gulls tilted in the hot air that was sewagey with the odour of low tide, swooped for the popcorn and ice cream wrappers overflowing the trash bins. There was the crushed glass glitter of the sea, the rumble of roller skates on wood, and the false ease and polite enquiries, and then the awkward hug he'd given David when they said goodbye and each side made its escape. It was worse that Helen changed the subject and did not refer to the meeting at all, because that left Greenberg imagining her thoughts, which he knew would be acute and detailed and damning. She did say one thing, later, hours later, in the evening in a lounge overlooking the sea, she said that he had so much history, and he knew with-

172 / ATOMIC ROAD

out asking exactly what she referred to: his son, his ex, all that baggage, as if these things were slowing him down while she needed to speed up. He argued, he debated, he showed her how she was wrong, but she was right and they both knew it.

He pulled the blanket up over his head, yet still saw the flame through the fabric, so he clenched his eyes shut and wished Jean Claude would hurry and get things over with.

☙❧

He fell into a reverie, half dream half delusion, a dark corner of his mind in a dark corner of his mind, a room within a room where he found a collection of deaths posed like the wax effigies in Madame Tussauds. Here was deaf Beethoven resting his head on the piano that he might feel his own music in his skull. Here was Frans Hals freezing to death in his room at eighty-two because he couldn't afford a shovel full of coal. There was Joyce blind in one eye and palsied with syphilis. Van Gogh sat twisted in despair. Melville hunched and forgotten. Hemingway by his own gun, and only two months ago Faulkner. Gone, gone, all the real men, the artists of apocalypse, gone. Keats and Rimbaud, De Quincey wide-eyed and dreaming, Gericault, Delacroix, Goya, and Rembrandt, yes, Rembrandt looking at him from out of those eyes that cradled his death like an infant.

☙❧

"Greenbairg..." Jean Claude was peering down. "Come up, Greenbairg."

He stood, wobbled, gripped the ladder rung to steady himself and slowly began to climb. How much nobler to be climbing to his death than descending. Forearm all but useless, he clung with his elbow. When he reached the top, Jean Claude grabbed him under the armpits and hauled him to his feet. Greenberg fought to find a balance between dignity and defiance. There would be no grovelling. Jean Claude slapped Greenberg's right cheek and then his left. But lightly, fondly, and what was this: Jean Claude was grinning. He stepped forward—Greenberg winced—and embraced him. Then Jean Claude thrust him away though held him above the elbows, in the manner of comrades, old campaigners, friends who shared an unbreakable bond, his expression wide and sympathetic. He was clean shaven and wore a wool-lined denim jacket and a checked wool shirt and work boots. He released Greenberg and slung an arm around his shoulders and walked him out of the barn into the snow and the light which stung his eyes, past the crows that sat in respectful silence in the tree, on toward the house whose windows glowed warmly in the afternoon.

For the next hour Jean Claude described LSD, the infinities glimpsed in the swirling patterns of each fingertip, the sensation of his fingernails growing at the rate of tropical bamboo, the intimacy of his feet upon the earth, the miracle of gravity, the realization that anger was poison, that ice, water and air were the three faces of eternity, that the mayfly was immortal, that money was piss, and that time flowed like a river in perpetual flood even as his thoughts raced along the bank in an endearing if ludicrous effort to describe it, to encapsulate it, to own it, and he laughed as he circumambulated the table, pausing by the stove and holding his hands out as though calling forth the power of heat: "This is good," he said, "this is very good." And all the while the snow fell white and silent and Wanda's Baoding balls tinged like the bells of a shrine and Madeleine looked on.

❦

The Packard handled well. The snow was five inches deep and packed by a night and a day of tires. Jean Claude had strapped on a set of tire chains that now slapped as the wheels went around. But the old car ran with a sureness that could almost make Greenberg believe the vehicle possessed the memory of a war horse that had seen far worse.

As he passed Smokey's he slid low in the seat and accelerated. The rental Dodge was gone, no doubt retrieved, along with those two bottles of Scotch, by some Hertz flunky.

He was heading back up to Minot, intending to catch Highway 52 to Fargo and then carry on down to Chicago. From there he might just leave the car and fly to New York. When he reached Minot he looked for a bank. He was down to his last ten dollar bill. Driving slowly through the icy streets he saw the Shell station where he'd talked to the kid. He pulled in alongside the restrooms and went in and washed his hands and face in hot water. Hot water on a cold day in a public toilet. Yankee genius. Sure, the kid in the gas station would go off on his world tour—but he'd return relieved to be an American.

Greenberg leaned on the sink and looked at himself. A scribble of hair atop his balding skull, strong eyebrows, his injured eye clearing up nicely, bold nose, the full lips of a good lover, a good chin—the cleft adding character—what a difference it made to be stress-free. And he'd shown mettle. He'd proved he had balls. He'd been in not one but two bomb shelters, hunted, trapped, wounded—struck with a shotgun—and stood his ground, didn't whimper or wilt, or not too badly … It was the rapprochement with Jean Claude that buoyed him most. "Greenbairg," he'd said, "keep your art and your money. You must go to Weyburn and try LSD. You will thank me." He wanted Madeleine to do the same, said he'd go with her, they'd do it together. "We will visit God!" She'd called him an idiot but had been smiling. When Greenberg was getting into the Packard she'd actually given him a brief hug. He gave them his address in New York and insisted they drop in if they were ever in town and he almost meant it.

Now, drying his hands on a paper towel, he decided he would drive all the way home because it would give him the peace and quiet to plot out his novel. A couple of chapters and an outline would snag a fat advance. Then knock off the rest in Spain or Italy or Morocco, somewhere warm. He shivered. He hated winter. The story was all there except the ending. Maybe it didn't need an ending. Endings were passé and so were beginnings, were we not stuck in the gears grinding time? Either way, it was a happy story, everything had worked out, sort of, and now, right now, he was in the curious position of experiencing his own denouement.

He stepped outside. The snow had stopped and wind scraped the pale grey cloud exposing high hard blue. Cars passed slowly on the icy road then idled as the signal went from amber to red and exhaust rolled like the aftermath of an explosion.

Greenberg pulled open the glass door looking for the kid. Had he already left for South America? Maybe Greenberg could take David with him to Europe and show him France and Spain, the Louvre and the Prado, maybe dip on down to Morocco and see Marrakech. Get close, father and son, it was long overdue and not too late, no, not too late at all. Yes, as soon as he got back to New York he'd contact him.

The Halloween decorations were gone and a different boy was behind the counter. This kid was bigger, thicker, but nervous, and he watched Greenberg warily. On the wall beyond him rows of cigarette packs formed a background: Kent, Camel, Marlboro, Old Gold, Pall Mall. They resembled decorative ceramic tiles; when their repeating patterns began to whisper Warhol, he shook his head. The kid continued to stare, and Greenberg became conscious that they were not alone, that there was someone behind a revolving wire book rack. He read the titles: *Ship of Fools, Franny & Zooey, Seven Days in May*. And Bob. Wearing the same shiny green jumpsuit zipped to the throat, though now, due to the weather, sporting a black Tyrolean hat with a red and gold feather as well as a matching red and gold scarf. Was there a flicker of a smile on Bob's face? Did Bob register joy? He slid sideways as if on casters and when he reached the door he turned the lock. It slid to with a metallic finality. He looked at Greenberg for a moment, during which he seemed to evaluate the evidence, consider the circumstances, their particular history, the time, the place, the options, and after having weighed all of this to gauge the appropriate next move, then—and only then—he looked to the kid behind the counter and said in his velvet monotone that betrayed just a hint of triumph, just an echo of delight, "Call Swen."